RAVENTREE HOLLOW

RYAN HOYT

For Shirley and Stephen, who showed me how to find the humanity in fear, and the fear in humanity.

And for my mom, who always made sure I had books to read, even if they gave me nightmares.

Chapter One

A scream pierced the veil of silence on a muggy July night. A rolling set of crashes and tumbles accompanied it. It was five seconds at most, but by the end, Agnes Butterfield was certain she had yanked half the village out of their slumber. She wasn't even worried about herself, sprawled out at the bottom of the stairs, an armful of pots scattered around her. She didn't think about the bone protruding at an unnatural angle from just above her right ankle. Nor the blood coming from her mouth where she'd bitten her tongue on the way down. Nor the crimson that soaked her snowy white hair where her scalp had been sliced open on the edges of the stairs.

Damn foolish woman, she thought to herself, *now you'll be the talk of the town, waking half the village like that.* Her pain was a distant second to the embarrassment she knew was coming. And her breath! *Oh yes, my breath. They'll know about the drink from my breath. I must cover it.*

The crumpled wreck of a woman tried to sit up, but her vision filled with imaginary stars. She lay down and attempted to slide on her back toward the kitchen. She bent her right knee, set her dangling foot on the ground, and applied force. That was when the pain became real to her, the brokenness of her body overcoming the shame in her mind.

A shrill scream of "Help me!" emanated from the frail lump on the ground of the Raventree Inn. Had the inn actually housed any guests that night, surely they would have heard the initial scream when she'd fallen. But it was the middle of a Tuesday night, and there were never visitors on Tuesdays in their little town, which was far off the path any well-to-do travelers would take for business or pleasure. And so Agnes Butterfield screamed a few more times before resigning herself to the darkness that overtook her. Her last thoughts were a jumble of *What will they think of me? They'll laugh at me!* and *This is the worst pain I've ever felt. I think I'm dying!*

But frankly, it was the shame she worried about most.

HER EYES OPENED, BUT IT TOOK GREAT EFFORT TO keep them open for more than a few seconds. Initially, all she saw was a cloudy white all around her, accompanied by horrible pain from the top of her head down to her mangled right foot. There was dizziness mixed in that she recognized from her mornings after the bottle, and in that moment she regretted her thirst for the stuff more than ever before. Sure, it wasn't *so* bad on its own when she could just rise in the morning and make herself a strong pot of black coffee. But to feel this way and be unable to move was not something she ever wanted to experience again. She tried again to separate her eyelids, and this time she grunted as she did it.

"Quite the spill you had, Ms. Butterfield." A calm voice spoke out from somewhere in the room. "You'll feel a little lightheaded; I had to give you something for the pain and to keep you asleep while I set some of your bones and stitched you up in several places."

She knew that soft voice, and she despised it. It belonged to one of the town's two doctors, Dr. Kenneth Chou. *Oh, why did he have to be the one I was sent to? Why, oh why? Oh, the shame.* It wasn't that he was a horrible man, at least not as far as she'd been able to learn from the rumor mill. And she'd tried, believe it—she'd tried to find dirt on the doctor, something good and juicy, but she just couldn't. That's what upset Agnes Butterfield. She could find faults in every person she came across, but Dr. Chou's faults had always eluded her. And it wasn't because he was... *ethnic*. No, Agnes didn't have a racist bone in her body.

Really!

There were many people of color in town whom she got on with perfectly well. There was... who was there? Oh yes—the Lamanna family lived on a farm just outside of Raventree Hollow, and their children were so precious. Italians, they were. And then the Duarte family, who owned one of the three restaurants in town. They were from somewhere down near Mexico, maybe Texas. She even recommended that guests at her inn eat at their establishment when they asked! And of course there was the young lord himself, Phillip Winfield, in the estate above Raventree Hollow. His grandmother had been an African woman whom old Horace Winfield had met and married during an expedition to that far-off continent, and what a scandal *that* had been in Raventree Hollow, according to old Grandmother Butterfield. But the Winfield family was beloved. They were good to the people in town, and nobody held young Phillip's ancestry against him in these modern times!

But back to Dr. Chou—just *what* was he hiding?

"My vision is coming back to me, Doctor," Agnes said, her voice horrifyingly muffled. She tried to reach up with her right arm, but it was then that she noticed the sling it was in. She tried her left arm instead, and it worked. Agnes reached up to her mouth and felt her swollen lip. Gauze filled her cheeks to keep her from biting her stitches. "I don't like the way I feel."

"Yes, well, you're going to feel worse if we take you off the morphine. I think this is the best regimen considering all that you're dealing with. You broke bones in your right arm and your right foot. I had to stitch up the crown of your head and your lip, tongue, and inner cheek. And then there's the bruising just about everywhere."

Agnes reached up and felt the top of her head. She screamed, perhaps louder than she had when she'd fallen. A huge patch of hair was gone.

"What did you do?" she cried, gauze hanging halfway out of her mouth. "What did you do to me?"

"I'm sorry, Ms. Butterfield, but I couldn't stitch up the wound without shaving some of your hair away. It was imperative in order to—"

"You horrible man," she interrupted. "What will they think of me? I can't believe you did this to me! I want Dr. Marshall!"

"I can assure you, Ms. Butterfield, that Doc Marshall would have done the same thing," said Dr. Chou, his voice remaining as gentle as always. "It really was necessary. It was too large a wound to leave alone. You're in expert hands here, and Doc Marshall is out of town with his wife this week, anyway. Now, please rest. I've got to see to another patient, and you need the sleep."

Agnes couldn't remember why she'd been digging through her attic in the first place. She hadn't needed those heavy items she'd been carrying down the stairs. There weren't any guests at her inn to cook for, nor any planned social gatherings. It hurt her head just attempting to remember what she'd been doing before the fall. It was as if she wasn't in control of herself, like something was blocking her memories. She had blacked out from alcohol many times before, but something felt different this time.

Agnes cried herself into another cycle of sleep, though it was anything but restful. She had dream after dream of people talking about her, laughing, pointing. Had someone else in town suffered these injuries, Agnes would already have started a whisper network. *I heard she was drinking,* she would've told her friend Ronnie Marie Jennings, *sucking at that bottle like a fish on land. Pathetic little thing.* And Ronnie Marie would've told Alexandra Pennington at the flower stand on Main, who would've spread it to her customers, like Connie Weathers, the barber's wife, who would've told her husband, Frank, who would've spread it to his clients during their morning clip-and-shaves. And then it would've been whispered to Howard Gibson, the banker, and his secretary, Lydia

Calhoun, who would've told her best friend, Melissa Rosenbaum, who would've—

I must do something about this, Agnes Butterfield thought when her eyes popped open sometime that evening in the recovery room. *They all know by now, surely, but there must be a better story out there, and then they'll forget about me entirely.*

Despite the pain, a crooked smile formed on her purple-and-blue face as Agnes Butterfield schemed.

Chapter Two

Eggs and toilet paper. Eggs and toilet paper! Oh, why did it have to be eggs and toilet paper?

Like every morning, Alexandra Pennington had come out to the stall in front of her house on Main Street only minutes after sunrise. Her routine was to wipe away any new webs the wretched spiders in her yard had formed during the night, woven between the slats of her picket fence and among the rows of flowers. Then she would unlock the door and windows of the stall, take inventory of the paper and lace she used to wrap flowers for her customers, and stock the cashbox so she'd have correct change readily available. Finally, she would prepare her standing orders so they'd be ready for her regular customers' early pickups.

But this morning, it was eggs and toilet paper she had to worry about. Alexandra shook with rage but stifled a scream so as not to draw attention, just in case any of the local business owners were out early to open up their own shops.

"Who would do such a thing?" Alexandra asked nobody in particular as she got to work, carefully pulling dew-soaked toilet paper bits out of her precious roses in one corner of the garden. She pondered the question as she scrubbed slimy yellow yolk off of the fence that lined the sidewalk of the town's primary business district. She tried to go as fast as she could so she'd finish before any customers arrived, but she feared that the paint would rub off her fence if she was too careless.

"Varsity training camp started yesterday," a boy's voice chirped behind her. Alexandra jumped at the sound of it, then turned, embarrassed, to face Arnie McCann. She should have expected him to pass by on his way to the library; the fourteen-year-old held a key and a volunteer title because he was there so often that he'd started picking up responsibilities. He had walked past Alexandra every morning this summer at the crack of dawn, usually with arms full of books, as if he didn't get his fill all day long in the stacks.

Alexandra didn't respond. She just stared at him, trying to control her breathing, trying not to let her rage show. He stared back, scratching at the pimples on his chunky cheeks just under his thick-framed spectacles. Once Arnie had scraped off enough of the growths on his face, he wiped his fingers on his sleeveless argyle sweater and spoke again.

"Every August, the varsity football team goes out after their first day of practice and tears up the town. Yours is the third house I've seen today that got trashed like this."

The boy didn't wait for a reply this time. He turned and resumed his journey up Main Street. Alexandra recalled hearing about incidents like this in the past, but she had never been a victim of the high schoolers' pranks herself. *Someone has to take care of that coach*, she thought. *He lets this go on year after year, and it's just not right!*

After her hard scrubbing had removed all the egg, Alexandra ran to the shed behind her house and found a leftover can of paint from when she had refinished her fence in the spring. She had just finished the last touch-up when she smelled a hint of cologne from behind her. She turned and looked up at the approaching man.

"Mr. Winfield," she croaked in shock. "Uh, I mean, good morning, sir! I was just tidying up a bit. Please, mind the wet paint!"

"Let me give you a hand with that," Phillip said. The young man reached down for the lid on the sidewalk, set it on the paint can, and pounded on it to seal it shut.

"Why, thank you, Mr. Winfield!" Alexandra hoped she was using her most sincere voice and not displaying the humiliation she felt. She led him through her garden and back toward the shed to put away the paint. She nervously glanced around, hoping she had removed every sign of the eggs and toilet paper that had been used to vandalize her beautiful garden. "It's not every day we see you downtown. To what do we owe the pleasure?"

"Oh, I just came by to see what flowers were in season. I have a guest from the big city coming to the house this afternoon and wanted to have some fresh-cut flowers out."

"The house," he says so modestly. If that's just a house, then my home may as well be a crate in the alleyway.

"Well, I can put together a nice bouquet for you now that you've helped me put away this paint. So kind of you to come here to my establishment when I know you have exquisite gardens up on your estate." The Winfield estate certainly did have beautiful gardens and a full-time gardener Alexandra despised. Oh, it wasn't personal, just principle.

"Yes, but you know Franz, Ms. Pennington. One can't even pick a single petal without giving him an anxiety attack."

"Please, tell me about this guest, and I'll pick out just the right combination to match him."

"*Her*, actually," Phillip said. This piqued Alexandra's interest, but she tried not to show it. "Very sweet young lady—a real go-getter, you know. Fiery red hair. Um, green eyes, I think. Is that the kind of thing you want to know?"

"Perfect!" In reality, she didn't care how the woman looked, as there were only so many flowers in her garden to choose from at this time of year; she was just looking for more information she could share. Information was currency in this town, and it would surely distract people from the story about her garden getting vandalized by those varsity football rascals. And what juicy information this was. The woman sounded absolutely nothing like Phillip Winfield's recent gal, who hadn't been seen in quite some time.

"Now, why don't you give me about twenty minutes," Alexandra said. "I'll have quite the bouquet made up for you in the time it will take you to go grab a cup of joe over at Graham's Diner. He should have a fresh pot on right now, in fact."

"You got it," Phillip said, a drop of morning dew from a tree shining in his auburn curls. He flashed his genuine, pearly white smile, turned, and walked out the gate and down the street.

Alexandra forgot all about the eggs and toilet

paper. As she used her shears to clip the perfect flowers, she began to formulate the story she would tell the whisper network. She wondered who might come along next this morning. Oh, she'd have to wait until after Phillip had picked up his order, of course, but perhaps Teresa White would be along shortly, or maybe even Bill Cunningham. This story would have legs, surely—Phillip Winfield with a *new* special lady friend, plus whatever that meant for the *old* special lady friend! Something this exciting only happened once in a blue moon in Raventree Hollow.

THE SQUEAK OF THE WHEELCHAIR GAVE AWAY THE identity of Alexandra's next visitor before she even saw the woman's face. Ever since that nasty fall down the stairs three weeks ago, Agnes Butterfield had been confined to the chair. Poor Shirley Bettencourt's mother had volunteered her to help wheel Agnes around town, and Shirley was too soft-spoken to push back against her mother's orders. Alexandra peered out from the booth as she finished wrapping and tying the bundle of flowers for Mr. Winfield.

"Well, a beautiful morning to you, my lovely dear Agnes," she said in her most sugary voice; she winced at her own disingenuousness, which surely bled through. "You're just glowing this morning. It looks as if you're healing nicely."

"Hello, Al," Agnes grumbled. *Al*—Alexandra simply *hated* being called Al, and Agnes knew it. Agnes turned to Shirley. "Leave me here, girl. Get yourself a muffin, but better make it bran. At least the fiber will do you some good."

Agnes rummaged through her purse and pulled out a handful of coins, which she dropped into Shirley's hands. The girl uttered a soft "Thank you, ma'am," and scurried off toward the neighboring Graham's Diner.

On the list of people Alexandra had hoped to see this morning, Agnes Butterfield was among the lowest. While small-town boredom fueled most of the whispering in Raventree Hollow, Agnes seemed motivated by something else: a pure hatred toward her neighbors, perhaps. Then again, Alexandra knew that if ever there was someone who could spread a story fast, it was Agnes.

"I know that look," Agnes said from her wheelchair, just inside Alexandra's gate. "You're holding out on me. That's quite a lovely bouquet you're preparing. Someone have a hot date? Who's been here this morning?"

"Well, if you must know..." Alexandra said, a sly smile forming across her face. She turned and looked toward the diner to make sure the subject of her gossip wasn't approaching before continuing. "Our young lord has a lady friend whose arrival is imminent. He wanted something really special prepared for her."

"Lady friend?" Agnes reached up to adjust the shawl wrapped around her head. She hadn't shown anyone, but everyone knew Agnes was missing chunks of hair after getting stitched up after her drunken tumble. The swelling on the woman's face had mostly gone down, though her lip still had quite the blackened scab and Alexandra was certain that Agnes's nose was more crooked than ever. "Would this be the same lady friend as before? I thought she fell off the face of the earth, it's been so long."

"A new one," Alexandra said. She thought back to a few minutes prior. Phillip had only said she was a guest from the big city and that she had fiery red hair, but that was good enough; Alexandra could read between the lines and even embellish a little. "He's very much in love with this one; I'm fairly certain wedding bells are in their future, from the sound of it. She's a real beauty. Bit of a ginger, too. He just gushed over her, blushing and all."

"Well, I just knew it wouldn't work out with that other gal he was seeing. She looked like trouble, you know. Um, I don't mean because... well, you know."

Yes, Alexandra knew what Agnes was getting at. Mr. Winfield's previous steady was Black, and Agnes had let her scorn be known to anyone who would listen, though she always made a point to sound like it was anything but the color of the woman's skin that she disliked.

Agnes continued with a smile, trying to recover. "A redhead? Now, isn't that something? Just wait until I tell the girls."

"Oh yes, well—"

"And you said she's arriving today?"

"Yes, that's what Phillip—Mr. Winfield—said. I'm just finishing up this bouquet, and he'll be along shortly to pick it up for her."

"Good, good. Say, if Shirley comes out looking for me, tell her I'm on my way down to see Connie and that I won't need her again until noon. Take care, now."

Agnes reached down to the wheels, guided the chair back to the sidewalk, and turned in the direction she had just come from minutes earlier. Before she wheeled away, she called out to Alexandra, "You missed a spot of toilet paper hanging from your roof, dear," and rolled on without looking back.

As if on cue, Phillip Winfield came out of the diner to pick up his flowers. He thanked Alexandra, paid and tipped generously, flashed his dazzling smile, and went on his way back up to the manor. As she watched him go, guilt flushed through her. She'd participated in the gossip game many times before, but something felt unsettling this time. Involving Phillip's personal life in it was like biting the hand that feeds.

What was I thinking? she wondered. But then, she didn't remember thinking at all. The words had just come out as if she hadn't chosen to speak them. It was almost as if something had taken control of her from the moment she'd seen the eggs and the toilet paper.

As Phillip Winfield made his trek up the eastern hill toward his sizable estate, the birds began to sing their morning songs. By the time he arrived at his front door, word of his new lover had already spread throughout the town.

Except, of course, this mystery girl wasn't his new lover at all. But what did facts matter to the people of Raventree Hollow when the story was just so juicy the way they told it?

Chapter Three

Shirley Bettencourt opened the front door to her family's home—like the rest of Raventree Hollow, it was never locked—and stepped inside, not even bothering to close the door behind her.

"Shirl, is that you?" Her mother called from the bathroom as Shirley floated past on the way to her bedroom. "What are you doing back so soon? You didn't get fired from another job, did you?"

"Yes, Mother, it's me," Shirley said in a dreamy tone. "Ms. Butterfield sent me away for the morning. Wanted privacy, I guess."

Shirley closed the door to her bedroom, which she often did keep locked. She dropped her purse next to the door and sank down into the accent chair with a sigh of satisfaction. She looked around at the walls of her room, where there hung corkboards covered in photos and newspaper clippings. If one were to get past the locked door of Shirley Bettencourt's bedroom, one would think the nineteen-year-old had a bit of an unhealthy obsession with Phillip Winfield, the young master of the Winfield estate on the eastern hill that overlooked Raventree Hollow. And one wouldn't be mistaken, what with all the pictures she had taken during high school and developed in the photography class's darkroom, and with all the newspaper articles she had so delicately cut out of the *Raventree Herald* for as long as she could remember. Her mother knew, but she told herself that her daughter just had a deep interest in local news. Nothing was more newsworthy to the town than the generous and wealthy Winfield family heir.

Shirley inhaled deeply and released her breath slowly as she recalled her close encounter with Phillip just minutes earlier. He'd been sitting at the counter at Graham's Diner, sipping his coffee, when she had walked in. She could have stood in the doorway and stared at him for several minutes if it hadn't been for those darn bells on the door, which had caused old man Graham to look up at her and in turn led Phillip to turn and flash his smile at her. She had felt flames rise in her cheeks instantly and had cast her eyes down to the ground as she'd plopped into the booth nearest the door. From behind the counter, old man Graham had called out to Junior to wait on Shirley.

Shirley despised Graham Herndon Jr. They'd been in the same class at school, and he had always teased her, from preschool through the day they'd walked across the gymnasium stage to accept their diplomas. A few of their classmates had gotten out of Raventree Hollow for college, but unfortunately, Shirley still had to see Junior around town regularly.

"Hiya, Shirl," Junior had greeted her loudly, sounding unusually cheerful. He'd dropped a menu on the table for her and flashed his big, crooked grin. He'd made no effort to lower his voice as he continued, "Say, you're looking mighty flushed this morning. Is everything all right?"

"I, um, yes, thank you, everything is fine," Shirley had mumbled as she'd shot a glance toward Phillip at the counter; he had gone back to sipping his coffee and chatting with old man Graham. She'd winced as she realized Junior had followed her gaze.

"Why, Shirley Bettencourt," Junior had chided. His beady little rat eyes had somehow gotten more beady and rat-like as his typical malicious expression reformed on his face. "Still got your eye on the prize, eh? You sure you don't want to sit at the counter? You'd have some good company!"

Shirley had wondered if Phillip and old man Graham were staring at her at that moment—she could have sworn their gazes were stabbing her like tiny daggers—but she had just lifted the menu to block her face and pretend to read the breakfast specials.

"Just a blueberry croissant and a glass of water, please," she had uttered from behind the menu. Junior hadn't pushed her further, only walked back to the counter to prepare her order. A moment later, she'd heard Phillip Winfield drop some coins on the counter, thank the Grahams, and walk toward the door. As she'd listened for the bells, she had once again thought she felt eyes on her. That's when she had known that Phillip Winfield was hesitating right behind her at the door. He had seen her. He wanted to reach out to her, to tell her "Good day," to kiss her goodbye. She just knew it.

Phillip Winfield loved her as much as she loved him.

"SHIRLEY," HER MOTHER CALLED THROUGH THE locked door as the knob rattled. "Ms. Butterfield rang. She said she is ready for luncheon. Shirl? What are you doing in there?"

"Just resting, Mother. I'll be out in a moment." Shirley was briefly disappointed to be awoken from her mid-morning nap, especially given the nice dream she'd been having about Phillip Winfield sweeping her away to the coast for a romantic weekend. But such dreams were normally dashed, weren't they? What else were mothers for but to bring their daughters back to reality?

Shirley smoothed her skirt as she approached the door. Her mother was still giving the locked door-knob stilted turns from the other side. "All right, Mother, I'm up now."

Shirley opened the door and faced her mother. It was almost like looking in the mirror, or maybe one of those funny mirrors at the county fair that passed through town every June, the kind that stretched you out one way and squished you down another way. This invisible mirror was one that aged you about thirty years, covered you in wrinkles, and greyed your hair. There was no denying that Shirley was Susan Bettencourt's flesh and blood, as much as Shirley used to fantasize about having been secretly adopted. The two women were strikingly similar with their athletic builds, their long, thin hair that was almost shapeless—Shirley often wished she had the rich, wavy hair of many of the girls she attended school with—and pale, freckled skin that reddened easily from embarrassment, sun, or pretty much anything else.

"Is Ms. Butterfield treating you well, dear?"

"Oh, I suppose she's treating me well enough, but she's just so unpleasant to be around all the time. I really don't see how you put up with her at those bridge games you and the other women play."

"She's just lonely, what with her husband abandoning her and leaving her with that old, run-down hotel," her mother said. Shirley was certain she spotted a tinge of guilt on her mother's face for pushing her to work as an assistant for the wretched Agnes Butterfield. "Plus, you need something to do, and she needs the help. It's only until she's able to walk again, two or three more months at most."

"If Dad would just let me work for him at the paper, I wouldn't need something to do."

"That's enough, Shirley," her mother said. She led Shirley out to the kitchen, where she thrust a hunter-green lunch box toward the girl. "Now, I want you to drop off your father's lunch on your way back over to Ms. Butterfield's place. Hurry up, Agnes is waiting for you."

Shirley took her father's lunch, which she assumed was his normal mix of leftovers, cold cuts, and a bottle of pop. It wasn't likely that the box contained any fresh produce. If it wasn't canned corn or candied apples, her father didn't consume any vegetables or fruits.

As she stepped off the porch, Shirley realized she had left her bicycle at Ms. Butterfield's inn that morning. She hadn't planned on coming home so soon. So she headed on foot back down Sycamore Avenue toward Main, cutting across Third to bypass Graham's Diner; if she had to see Graham Junior one more time that day, Shirley thought she'd be sick.

She arrived at the office of the *Raventree Herald*, its front window emblazoned with the paper's title in an oversize gothic font; smaller, plainer letters spelled out HAL BETTENCOURT, EDITOR IN CHIEF below it. The door swung open as she reached for the handle.

"Hiya, Shirley!" In the doorway stood a tall, gangly young man with childish blond hair and what a seventh-grade boy might call a mustache. He was wheeling out a silver bicycle with a basket in the front. A camera with a large flashbulb hung from a strap around his neck. Pinned on his tweed jacket was a badge that read PRESS.

"Oh, good afternoon, Herman," Shirley said. "Your mustache looks like it's coming in just fine." She heard a tinge of disingenuousness in her voice; she didn't mean to be unkind, but she couldn't think of anything nice to say with more sincerity.

"Why, thank you!" Herman Stanley put his fingers to his upper lip and caressed the peach fuzz that resided there. "I'm off to Cherry Street. The varsity team hit old Jim Mertz's house last night, and he called it in. He's out for Coach Franklin's head and wants everyone to know about it. They got his house two summers in a row with toilet paper."

"That's Raventree Hollow for you," Shirley said. "Probably the biggest news we'll have all month."

"Say, why don't you come with me? I'll give you my camera, and you can snap some pictures while I interview Mr. Mertz. We both know you're the better photographer."

"That's awfully kind of you, Herman, but my father wouldn't dream of giving me credit in his paper, and he'd probably have your job over it," Shirley said.

Herman was right, of course. Shirley was a far superior photographer. Back in high school, the photography teacher, Mr. Hanley, had regularly featured Shirley's photos at the front of the class, whether they were pictures of nature or school events. He had always cited her as the example the rest of the class, including Herman, should follow. But when school ended and Shirley had floated the idea of working for her father at the paper, she had gotten only cold rejection from the man. Instead, he had hired her inferior former classmate, a sharp blow to Shirley.

"Hurry it up, Shirl," an icy voice boomed from

inside the office. "I have deadlines, and my lunch break should have been over by now. Off you go, Mr. Stanley; Mertz is waiting for you."

Herman flashed an embarrassed smile at Shirley. He placed his camera gently in the bicycle's basket and rode away toward his appointment on Cherry Street. Shirley entered the newspaper office and faced her father.

"Sorry it's late, Daddy," Shirley said, handing over the lunch box. "I'm off to Ms. Butterfield's for the afternoon."

"Shirl, I'm sorry I raised my voice just then," her father said. "It's just that readership is down and ad sales are stagnant. Ever since the big city paper started getting brought in... It's just not right."

"It's okay, Daddy." Shirley leaned in and gave her father a kiss on the cheek before turning toward the door.

"We just need some exciting news in this town," her father said as she pulled it open. She knew what he meant. The high school football team having a night on the town after their summer camp was probably the most eventful thing that had happened in Raventree Hollow in weeks. The flower show in May had provided a few days' worth of news, as had the county fair in June. But compared to the stories in the big city paper—Ms. Butterfield was a subscriber, and Shirley read it daily at the inn while Ms. Butterfield ate lunch—Raventree Hollow had nothing going for it.

If only something wild would happen in this boring old place, Shirley thought.

Little did she know, things were about to get much more exciting in Raventree Hollow.

Chapter Four

Pastor Laurence Wolfram heard the first of the bells strike noon as he stepped out of the sanctuary of the Raventree Community Church with his sack lunch. As was his usual routine when the weather was nice, Laurence sat down on the top step and dug into the brown bag. Like all the church's resources in recent years, his personal budget was scant, and his lunch was far from luxurious. Peanut butter and boysenberry jam on stale bread—full of holes from the mold spots he had removed that morning—and two softening apples were on the menu today.

He looked over the town square that started at Main Street and ended at the steps of the church. The placement had once represented the role of faith in the community, the importance of the location where ladies' knitting groups and retiree bingo nights and parent-teacher association meetings were held during the week and where the finest of potluck lunches happened every Sunday. Once upon a time, at least. These days, Laurence was lucky if he had a single visitor before lunch and if more than a handful of pews were filled on Sunday mornings.

Pastor Laurence always waited for the twelfth chime of the bell before he thanked God for his food and consumed the contents of his brown bag. As the dozenth chime sounded, he closed his eyes and bowed his head.

"Heavenly Father," he said aloud, but then the chime of a thirteenth bell interrupted the prayer. He nearly dropped the sack lunch. A fourteenth chime rang out, though it sounded as if it had been struck with considerably less effort, merely an echo of the previous one. Laurence stood up, descended the stairs into the courtyard, and looked up toward the western hill that flanked Raventree Hollow, opposite the eastern rise that housed the Winfield estate.

Up on the western hill was the Convent of the Sisters of Mercy, the oldest building in the region, first constructed by European immigrants in the eighteenth century before Raventree Hollow was even a dream. It was a large, castle-like affair with towers and spires, built of brick and stone, and it even had a wall around the perimeter to keep out the indigenous population. The building housed an unknown number of elderly nuns, and they were almost entirely self-sufficient, growing their own food, raising livestock, and living without the luxury of electricity. The people of Raventree Hollow had very minimal contact with the convent, and there wasn't even a Catholic church in the town. Any Catholics in Raventree Hollow had to travel to the big city for Sunday Mass.

"Those penguins must be hitting the communion wine a little too hard up there," a voice chirped behind him. He turned to face Katrina Givens, the town witch. *Naturalist*, Laurence reminded himself. It was an easy mistake to make. The woman did offer a number of unusual foreign and pagan remedies, goods, and services at her place of business, which pointedly sat several blocks from Main Street. The patience of the townsfolk stretched only so far, after all.

"They are ladies of the faith, and I'm sure they just miscounted," Laurence retorted. He didn't want to give Kat the opportunity to knock his fellow believers. She was a *unique* woman in the eyes of the people of Raventree Hollow, nearly all of whom had once been part of his congregation. Sure, nearly all of the townsfolk still identified as Christians and even as members of Raventree Community Church. But with the exception of a handful of individuals, they only showed up when it suited them, usually around Christmas and Easter. They had certainly stopped tithing regularly. Laurence's own defaulted rent payments were proof of that.

"Well, I must say they creep me out, always locked away up there, not associating with the rest of the town," Kat said. "You're looking a bit pale, Larry. I can mix you up a bit of my vitality remedy back at the shop if you want. No charge for an old friend."

Laurence blushed at the nickname. He hadn't been called Larry since high school, and even those who had graduated with him twenty-six years prior had mostly shifted to calling him Pastor or Laurence when he had returned to town from his seminary training and started working with the church. They had all treated him with more formality than he had expected. They had stopped thinking of him as a friend they could shoot the breeze with or invite out for a drink at the pub. The women had stopped looking at him as the handsome young man he was, even those who had known him since childhood. Everyone, that is, but Kat Givens.

They had been close friends as children, despite the Givens family being outcasts. The Givens hadn't been members of the church, and they had filled their home with pagan idolatry. Laurence's parents had encouraged the friendship, convinced that the Wolframs could convert the Givens family. It had never happened, of course, and as the church's hold over the people of Raventree Hollow had relaxed over the years, Kat Givens had become just another person the residents smiled at one moment and whispered about the next.

"I'm feeling fine, Kat. I'm just—"

"Lonely and trying to understand your place in this changing town?" She rubbed Laurence's left arm as he smiled bashfully.

"Well, yes. You've always known me better than I know myself. I can't help but feel less relevant than ever in this place. When I took over the church from old Pastor Duncan, it was a pillar of the community. Now several days can pass without a single soul stepping through those doors. I don't know if it's me or if times have just changed. Maybe it's already time to step down and let someone else take over."

"Listen to me, Larry. The people of Raventree Hollow are lucky to have you here when they need you. But maybe those needs are not at the top of their minds right now. There's something else the people here thrive off of, a different kind of religion."

"What are you—"

"Gossip. They live for it. Who's dating whom, which lady used canned ingredients in her recipe for the June Chili Cook-Off, how often Frank the barber's unmentionables graze his clients while he's cutting their hair. Their little stories start off as whis-pers, but eventually they turn into roars."

"Where there is no wood, there the fire goeth out; where there is no talebearer, the strife ceaseth," Laurence muttered, looking off into the distance. He turned his gaze back to Kat. "It's a proverb, but the sentiment is all over the Bible."

"You know," Kat said, a devious smile forming on her face, "maybe if you spent more time around town with them, your presence would make them stop slandering each other. It might even draw them back into your church."

Laurence silently considered. As he turned to face Main Street, a reflection of the midday sun off the windows of the old convent on the hill caught his eye. He focused on the place, seemingly dead, a relic of the past. Then he looked back to his church, and a fear swept over him that it would soon meet the same fate as the monolith in the hills.

"Look! There are some of your folks now," Kat said, pointing across the courtyard. Melissa Rosen-baum, Cherie Smith, and Michael Hayworth were walking purposefully up Main Street. "A strange little group if ever I saw one: a young grade school teacher, a cranky old seamstress, and the purveyor of the town dump, all heading somewhere together. They sure look like kindling for a fire to me."

Laurence looked again at the towering convent

and shuddered. He turned back to Kat and held his arm out to her.

"What do you say we take a walk and get reacquainted with our neighbors?" Laurence asked. Kat winked at him and put her arm in his. They headed off together toward Main Street.

Chapter Five

Shirley stepped through the side door of the Raventree Inn so she could get to work straight away on Ms. Butterfield's lunch. The state of the kitchen startled her when her eyes adjusted to the dimness of the place compared to the bright August sun outside. It was not at all as she had left it that morning after she had made Agnes's usual cheese omelet and buttered toast.

The countertops were covered with filthy trays that had been used for the breakfast buffets back when the inn was an actual destination for travelers, many years before Shirley could possibly remember. Some had sat on the pantry shelves, stacked and collecting dust and crumbs and rodent waste, while others had been moved up to the attic along with most of the other cookware. Someone had collected all the trays, chosen the ones with the least mess caked onto them, and left the rest for Shirley to clean. Surrounding these were the skins and cores and pits of various fruits and vegetables, tins of biscuits, and bags of crisps. Freshly prepared snacks covered two shining trays.

Ms. Butterfield had company this afternoon.

Shirley caught the distinct sound of laughter, one that could only come from Connie Weathers. She gently pushed open the double swinging doors and peeked into what had once been the inn's dining hall. Sure enough, Connie sat to Agnes Butterfield's right. Filling up the rest of the room was everyone from the owner of the bank to the town's only barber. Even Pastor Wolfram was there with Katrina Givens, the woman most of the town referred to as his mistress—though Shirley knew better and quite admired Kat herself.

What an odd assembly, Shirley thought. She pulled the doors closed as gently as she had opened them but forgot about the creak they always made on the way back in.

"Shirley, is that you, dear?" Ms. Butterfield called out.

Shirley had no choice but to reveal herself. She picked up a tray containing a spread of crackers, sliced salami, assorted cheeses, and peeled cucumbers and backed through the door.

"Ah, Shirl, I see you've found one of the trays Connie helped me prepare in your absence. Please serve our guests, and then you may go clean up the little mess we made in our rush to start the meeting."

"I apologize, Ms. Butterfield. I didn't realize you were going to have company today."

Shirley set the tray down on the table next to another that had already been wiped out, only crumbs and residue left on its surface. She picked up the empty tray and surveyed the motley crew. They were chattering away excitedly as they snacked, and nobody seemed to even notice her as she tried to understand what all the conversations were about. Shirley hurried back toward the kitchen and had just pushed the doors open when she heard a name that stood out from the rest of the chatter.

Phillip Winfield.

She stopped in her tracks. Her Phillip Winfield? Well, not hers, really, but...

"Thank you, Shirley, dear," Ms. Butterfield's falsely sweet voice called out to her, showing that she wasn't wanted in the room any longer. Shirley continued into the kitchen, letting the doors swing closed behind her. She set the empty tray down and stood quietly at the doors, opening them just enough to see into the room with one eye.

"Well, it looks like everyone is here now, and well fed," she heard Ms. Butterfield say. Her charismatic tone was a stark contrast with her normal crabby voice, but then, it always was when Ms. Butterfield had gossip to share. It seemed to be the only thing the woman valued in her sorry, insignificant life.

"I'm sure some of what I'm about to tell you all has already reached your ears, but I want to be sure we're all on the same page," Ms. Butterfield went on. "This morning, a little birdie told me some very shocking news. As you know, the magnanimous Phillip Winfield, the sole heir of the fine family that has been a benefactor of this town for generations, was set to marry Rebecca Abrams, whom he met while he was away at college. In the two years since his return to his family's manor above our humble town, Ms. Abrams has visited quite regularly. Though of course, she never did stay here at the town's only inn. I'm ashamed to say it in front of the good Pastor Laurence here, but it appears that she spent the nights under the same roof as her fiancé."

Here Ms. Butterfield paused for dramatic effect, and Connie and others feigned shock with ridiculous gasps.

"Oh, it's no business of mine," the clergyman said. Shirley couldn't be sure, but she thought she heard a hint of ridicule in his voice.

Perhaps he and Kat only came for the entertainment, Shirley thought. They weren't usually the types to take part in these gatherings of crows Ms. Butterfield sometimes held.

"Well," Ms. Butterfield continued, "we haven't seen Ms. Abrams here in town all summer. Some of us were beginning to wonder what had happened to their engagement. You know how fleeting adolescent love can be. So imagine my shock when the little birdie told me this morning about a new woman in Phillip Winfield's life! I don't know what Ms. Abrams did to break his heart, but it seems Mr. Winfield has managed to recover and is now set to marry a gorgeous new gal, one that must be more his type."

A collective sound of awe emanated from the group as the guests murmured amongst themselves.

"What do you mean by 'more of his type'?" Kat called out, breaking up the noise. Everyone hushed.

"Well, Ms. Givens, I just mean... you know..."

"His social class, of course," Connie offered. "The Winfields and others like them must hold themselves to different standards. Wealth and status, you understand."

"Yes, and I believe this fine new lady is well bred," Ms. Butterfield said in a pitch that was much higher than normal, which Shirley knew she only did when she was trying hard to cover a lie. "Equally yoked, as the good pastor might understand it."

"And when can we see this new young lady?" Howard Gibson asked with great interest.

"Why, she is coming to visit him today, according to my source!" This news provoked a round of *ooh*s and *aah*s from the crowd, and Shirley could just make out a smirk of satisfaction on Ms. Butterfield's face. The woman was holding her head higher than she had since her accident on the stairs a few weeks earlier. "And that is why I have gathered you all here today. We must do our best to welcome her to our town and ensure a successful marriage for our handsome and wealthy bachelor, Mr. Winfield."

Shirley backed away from the door and faced the mess in the kitchen. She thought back to the last time she had seen Phillip with Rebecca Abrams. It had been just before the county fair in June. Shirley had been out at the fairgrounds, a large meadow on the opposite side of the hill the Winfield estate rested on, just outside of town. She had been on one of her daily walks that had lasted entire afternoons back before she was stuck taking care of Ms. Butterfield. She had always brought her camera. The meadow had the most beautiful array of wildflowers in the late spring and early summer, at least until the fair moved in and everyone trampled the area until it was just a dry, dead patch of land.

And sometimes when she was out there, she *may* have ventured a little too high up the hill and into the back of the Winfield estate. And *perhaps* she had occasionally caught glimpses of Phillip pacing his gardens, chatting with the groundskeeper, Franz, or even sneaking kisses with his fiancée next to a fountain. In fact, Shirley *might* have had some photographs she'd taken of these scenes hanging on her bedroom walls.

Shirley remembered how happy and in love Phillip and Rebecca had seemed that last time she'd seen them together. The entire scene had felt like a long goodbye, but not a permanent farewell. Shirley had assumed Rebecca was going off to travel for the summer or perhaps to visit family in another part of the country. She couldn't believe the pair had broken up.

Ms. Butterfield must be wrong, she thought.

Shirley glanced up at the clock. It was nearing one in the afternoon. There was a train that arrived daily at half past one, and the station was just outside of Raventree Hollow.

Shirley walked past the dirty trays on the counter, headed out the side door, and grabbed her bicycle. Before she even thought about Ms. Butterfield's impending anger over the mess she had left behind, Shirley was halfway across town.

Chapter Six

Shirley hadn't quite reached the outskirts of town when she realized she didn't have her camera on her. She wanted to document the situation, but she certainly did not want to step foot in her house to grab her camera from her bedroom. She knew her mother would nag her about leaving Ms. Butterfield's side for the second time that day and pester her about what was going on.

"Herman!" she exclaimed as she hit the brakes on her bicycle at the corner of Main Street and Kings Valley Road. She made a U-turn and sped off toward Cherry Street.

Sure enough, she spotted the lanky young man on the sidewalk a few minutes later, snapping photographs of the soggy dangling toilet paper that decorated the trees and shrubbery in Mr. Mertz's yard.

"Two times now!" a man was shouting from the doorway of the house. "Two years in a row! Enough is enough. I want that coach and those kids to pay for this!"

As Shirley got closer to the house, she could see that Jim Mertz was holding the telephone. His veins were protruding from his forehead, and his knuckles were white from his grip on the receiver.

"He's been trying this whole time to reach the sheriff. Finally got him on the line." Herman snapped one more picture of the carnage and then let the camera dangle against his chest. He turned to Shirley with a hopeful smile. "Did you change your mind about covering the story with me?"

"I need to borrow your camera if you're done here," Shirley said without a greeting. "Please."

"What's going on? I think I got enough out of Mr. Mertz between his rants and his calls to the dispatcher. You should have heard the words coming out of that old man's mouth when he got Coach Franklin's wife on the phone, as if poor Judy Franklin had anything to do with—"

"Herman," Shirley interrupted, "can I borrow your camera or not?"

"Well, if it's so important, why don't I come with you?" The boy blushed. If there was anyone as transparent in their bashfulness as Shirley, it was the fair-skinned Herman Stanley. "That is, if it's acceptable to you."

"I don't have time for—" Shirley stopped herself and looked at the young man. She remembered how Carol Spencer and Mary-Ellen Norwick had teased her in school about Herman's unrequited love for her and how repulsed she'd been at the thought. It wasn't because Herman had done anything wrong; it was just the way those girls went on and on about it, as if Herman was so unattractive or unworthy. She hated herself for how she had treated him in high school... and how she had spoken to him just now.

"I'm sorry, Herman. Yes, you may come with me, but I don't have time to explain yet."

"Swell!" Herman said. He set his camera in his bike basket and waved to Mr. Mertz, who was still in the doorway. The old man growled some choice words into the receiver and made a gesture halfway between a wave and a *good riddance, thanks for nothing*. With that, Shirley and Herman sped off toward the train station.

THE KINGS VALLEY TRAIN STATION OUTSIDE OF Raventree Hollow was quite a quaint and rural affair. Shirley thought it must be an embarrassing locale for a rich man to meet anyone of his own ilk. She felt an odd sense of guilt on Phillip's behalf, as if the simple nature of the place made a statement about the man's own wealth, not to mention the small town the Winfield estate overlooked. What the locals considered the nearest big city had a much grander transportation hub, though Shirley could only imagine how it would pale in comparison with one in Paris or London or New York City. In those places, the sight of a Rolls-Royce pulling up, a chauffeur walking around to open the door, and an affluent and handsome young man stepping out and straightening his finely tailored clothing would have been commonplace. Here, outside of Raventree Hollow, it seemed absurd. Yet there was Phillip Winfield, standing at the curb in all his beautiful glory.

"What are we even doing here, Shirl?" Herman asked.

"Sit back down, and I'll tell you," Shirley responded.

They were on the platform at the station, bikes resting on their kickstands a few feet away from the bench where Shirley sat. Herman rejoined her on the uncomfortable seat, his arm gently grazing Shirley's by mistake. He quickly pulled away when she didn't react.

"The word in town is that Phillip left his fiancée for another woman and that this mystery woman is arriving on the next train. Can you get back up and pose?"

"Oh, um, sure," Herman responded. "How do you want me to stand?"

"I don't care, Herman, I'm not actually taking your picture." She regretted saying it as soon as the words left her mouth and she saw the defeated look on his face. "Sorry. What I mean is, I want to sneak some shots of Phillip behind you."

Shirley pointed the camera just to the left of Herman and zoomed in to get a better look at the object of her desire. His perfect teeth flashed as he broke into a dazzling smile. The skin around his eyes creased slightly and small dimples formed in his cheeks as he laughed at something his driver must have said. The warm breeze ever so slightly rippled the luscious waves of his hair. Shirley snapped a photograph and then continued to observe the man through the camera's viewfinder.

She noticed other things about him. He wasn't dressed as finely as he always had been when he and Rebecca were seen in public—or when Shirley had spotted them on the grounds of the estate. In fact, his clothes were completely informal, as if he were just running out to the market or lounging around at home. He didn't look at all like someone who was about to greet a new romantic partner, especially one he hadn't seen in quite some time.

No, something was off.

Shirley spotted Phillip checking his watch twice and growing agitated. He gestured impatiently to his driver.

"It's not a lover he's here to meet," Shirley said as she pulled the camera away from her face.

"How can you tell?" Herman asked.

"Trust me. I may not have a history of romance myself, but I know these things."

Shirley became even more convinced her intuition was correct when the train arrived. Only a handful of people got off, and Shirley recognized all of them—Ronnie Marie Jennings, the Brownings, and so on—except for one. The woman appeared to be in her mid-thirties, eight or ten years older than Phillip. Her clothes were more of a Neiman Marcus or Macy's style of fancy rather than custom-fitted, as Shirley would have expected of a wealthy woman. The luggage she carried didn't look like it had traveled to the Bahamas or the Riviera—instead, it was Greyhound chic.

Without being asked, Herman repositioned himself so that his back was facing the woman. Shirley brought the camera back up, aimed it just beyond Herman's right shoulder, and snapped photos of her as she set her bags down; the chauffeur approached her to pick them up and guide her to the car. Shirley saw only businesslike determination on the woman's face as she glanced at Phillip.

"I think I've got what I need for now," Shirley said a minute later as she snapped a final picture of Phillip and the woman shaking hands formally. She pulled the camera strap from around her neck and turned toward Herman. He was looking down at the ground, his hands in his pockets. "Herman, thank you for coming out here with me today and letting me use your camera. I'll come with you to develop the film."

"No," Herman said. "You should get back to the inn. I'm sure Agnes is wondering where you are."

"She'll be furious, no doubt about it."

"I'll get these developed and bring them to you tonight. Let's ride back into town. Your father is probably wondering why I took so long at Mr. Mertz's place."

"Well, the toilet paper probably *is* the biggest story of the week," Shirley quipped.

"Unless you've stumbled on something bigger here, Shirl."

Shirley thought about it. There didn't seem to be anything romantic between Phillip and the mystery woman, but Ms. Butterfield and her gabbing gang didn't know that yet.

Chapter Seven

"What did I tell you, Larry? They were practically glowing about you being there with them at that meeting."

"Is that really the right way to engage with the people of this town, though? I hate to look like I condone their behavior." Pastor Laurence had his doubts about the afternoon's activities, but he was on top of the world about spending so much time with Katrina Givens.

"I think your god will forgive you if even half of that room shows up in the sanctuary next Sunday." She reached for his hand and gave it a squeeze. Laurence wanted to grab hers and hold on. He wanted to guide her toward the fellowship hall inside the church and spend the rest of the day with her. But he knew better.

"Well, here we are. Would you like to come inside for a cup of tea? There are some leftover pastries from Sunday." He knew the answer before he even asked. Katrina Givens had not stepped foot inside of Raventree Community Church in all the years Laurence had been its pastor, and even the good time they'd had together that afternoon wasn't likely to break the streak.

"Thanks for inviting me, but I must get back to my shop. The note I left on the window said I'd be back by one o'clock. Until next time, old friend."

Laurence looked at her, wanting to speak words of reassurance, to tell her she wouldn't burst into flames the second she walked through the doors of the church, but he knew it wouldn't change anything. Kat flashed him one last smile and headed back toward Main Street. Laurence stood in the courtyard and watched her until she rounded a corner. Some of the others who had been at Agnes's meeting walked down the sidewalk behind Kat. They noticed Laurence and waved. He lifted his hand to return the gesture when a wave of guilt washed over him. He didn't understand it, but the rest of the proverb he'd recited to Kat that afternoon flooded into his mind:

As coals are to burning coals, and wood to fire; so is a contentious man to kindle strife. The words of a talebearer are as wounds, and they go down into the innermost parts of the belly. Burning lips and a wicked heart are like a potsherd covered with silver dross. He that hateth dissembleth with his lips, and layeth up deceit within him; when he speaketh fair, believe him not: for there are seven abominations in his heart. Whose hatred is covered by deceit, his wickedness shall be shewed before the whole congregation. Whoso diggeth a pit shall fall therein: and he that rolleth a stone, it will return upon him. A lying tongue hateth those that are afflicted by it; and a flattering mouth worketh ruin.

He turned to face his church, reluctantly determined to count that month's tithes and offerings and try to balance the books, when something caught his eye.

Up on the western hill, outside the wall that surrounded the Convent of the Sisters of Mercy, stood a flock of darkly clad women.

They were staring directly at Laurence.

Sure, from that distance, it was impossible to tell such a thing for sure, but Laurence was certain. He could feel it. Their unseen eyes bore a hole straight into his insides. Their gaze filled him with a deep shame. Laurence tore away from their grip and rushed up the steps into the sanctuary of his church.

Chapter Eight

"Oh, Ronnie Marie, I'm so glad you've come," Agnes Butterfield said.

Or slurred, more like.

She caught Ronnie Marie's glance at the whiskey bottle that was tucked in between Agnes's left thigh and the side of the wheelchair. Shame poured over her. It was her first time drinking since her little tumble a few weeks earlier. Or maybe the second, if she counted the evening she'd returned home from Dr. Chou's office, but she blamed that lapse on the painkillers. She brushed it aside; nothing would ruin this day for Agnes.

"Celebrating something, Aggie?" Ronnie Marie asked. She had entered the Raventree Inn to find Agnes lounging in front of the grandfather clock in the foyer, seemingly mesmerized by the relic.

"Yes, you just missed the big meeting. Everyone left only minutes ago. You should have seen them, Ronnie. I had them in the palm of my hand with my little exclusive story."

"And what story is that, dear? I've been out visiting Mother in the city, and I have a story myself. It involves—"

"Phillip Winfield and a new woman!" Agnes interrupted.

"Why, yes, how did you know?" Ronnie Marie was shocked. Agnes saw a wave of disappointment overtake the woman.

"Know what? That's my story. Phillip Winfield has a new special lady!"

"Yes," Ronnie Marie said. "I was about to tell you the same thing! I just came back from the city, and a woman I didn't recognize got off the train at our stop. And who was at the station to greet her?"

"Phillip Winfield, of course!" Agnes Butterfield gave a deep laugh, which turned into a coughing fit. Once she had composed herself again, she reached for her friend's hands. "Ronnie, you've seen her? Tell me, is she as gorgeous as Phillip said she is?"

"Well, I suppose so, but I do wonder if Phillip is having second thoughts about her already. When they greeted each other, it was awfully formal."

"Formal? Well, perhaps he was just being proper in a public place. Come, let's get some tea."

Ronnie Marie pushed Agnes's wheelchair down the hall and into the kitchen.

"What happened here?" Ronnie Marie asked with a start.

"Well, Connie helped me set up for the big meeting—there were a lot of folks here, I must say—and I didn't ask anyone to stay and help clean up afterward because I thought that no-good Shirley Bettencourt would be here to do it all."

"She was down at the station when I got off the train," Ronnie Marie said with smug satisfaction. It wasn't often that she got to one-up Agnes, but when she did, she reveled in it. "Don't know where your own helper is, eh, Aggie?"

"That's impossible! I saw her here at the start of our meeting. She served one tray, and then I sent her back to the kitchen. She was— That little witch! She was eavesdropping! She wanted to get the drop on me by seeing Mr. Winfield's new girl herself!"

"And she had a camera," Ronnie Marie snickered. "Pretending to photograph that dunce Herman Stanley. Boy, I tell you, Millicent and Robert Stanley created the dopiest little—"

The side door opened, and Shirley stepped into the kitchen. Her hair was windblown from speeding back on her bicycle, and she seemed out of breath. She looked nervously at Agnes and Ronnie Marie but put on a fake smile.

Agnes wasn't having it.

"You!" she screamed. She ignored the pain in her injured right foot and stood up from her wheelchair in anger. "Get out! Get out of here now!"

"I'm sorry, Ms. Butterfield," the girl muttered. Agnes knew immediately that she was terrified. "I just—"

"You were trying to get the drop on me, weren't you? And to think I employed you in my home, gave you a job when your own father didn't even want to put you to work! You ungrateful little wench. You're fired!"

"But I—"

"Out! Get out!"

The girl's mouth was agape. Shirley turned to Ronnie Marie as if expecting some support, but Agnes knew the woman was on her side. Ronnie Marie had been Agnes's closest friend since childhood. Tears formed in Shirley's eyes before she finally turned and ran out the door.

"Good riddance," Ronnie Marie said. She reached down, grabbed Agnes's whiskey bottle, and took a large swig. "You know, Aggie, you really shouldn't be drinking this stuff."

"Nothing's ruining my good day, Ronnie," Agnes said as she grabbed the bottle back and took a mouthful before dropping back into the chair with a wince of pain. "Absolutely nothing.

Be a dear and clean this mess up for your old friend."

Agnes Butterfield turned the chair and wheeled herself out of the kitchen, chuckling.

Chapter Nine

Tuesday had been a bad day, but Wednesday would be a better one. It just *had* to be.

Alexandra Pennington loved waking up early in the morning before most of the town was out and about, watching the sun rise over a new day, seeing the dew wash her flowers clean, smelling the pastries and coffee being prepared at the diner. Yes, today would be a better day.

Alexandra knew about Agnes's meeting at her little roach motel down the street even though that horrible woman hadn't invited her to attend. The gall of that woman! Spreading Alexandra's own piece of news, and certainly she hadn't given credit where it was due! Nobody had come by to thank Alexandra for the important piece of gossip that had gotten them all excited. But it was clear they were buzzing.

Everyone who had passed her stall that afternoon was whispering about Phillip Winfield's love life, but not one person had turned to her to talk about it. Even a pleasurable after-hours visit to Kenneth's office hadn't been enough to turn the day around, especially since she'd stumbled into Agnes's right-hand gal, Ronnie Marie, on the way back home. Had Ronnie Marie seen Alexandra exiting the good young doctor's practice? Had she told Agnes? If so, the news had surely been relayed to half the town by midnight.

Breathe, Alexandra thought to herself. *Just breathe.*

She opened her front door, ready to start fresh. Perhaps another bit of news would hit her ears and give her something else to think about. Surely some daydreams about her forbidden lover were bound to play in her head during the quieter moments of the day.

A wave of scents from her flowers poured over her as she stepped onto her porch. As she often did, Alexandra closed her eyes and breathed it in, smiling at the creations she labored over day in and day out. She was the most accomplished gardener in town. She was a successful businesswoman. She was an object of envy among those in town who wished to have thumbs as green as hers.

Alexandra cut her deep breath short. Something was not right—she could tell from the muddled scent. She opened her eyes and peered at her garden.

Eggs.

And toilet paper.

And not just eggs and toilet paper. Destruction. Her flowers had been trampled. Carnations. Roses. Daisies. Petunias. All of it—destroyed!

A scream left the woman's mouth and reverberated through the town.

She wasn't sure how long she stood there screaming before anyone responded. Finally, Graham Herndon Junior and Senior ran over from their diner.

"Miss Pennington, what is it?" the older man yelled in alarm. "What's the—"

"Oh my," the younger one exclaimed before breaking into nervous laughter. He quickly stopped, the awkward smile dying right on his stupid face as he saw the fury in Alexandra's eyes. "I didn't mean... it's just that..."

"You better have a look at this morning's paper, Miss Pennington," Graham Senior said. He picked up Alexandra's newspaper, which the delivery boy had tucked into the gate of the picket fence, and unrolled it. He walked through the trash heap that was Alexandra's precious garden and made his way up to the porch.

Alexandra yanked the newspaper out of the man's hands and read the headline out loud, doing her best to control her voice.

"'Varsity Team Strikes Again; Mertz Wants Coach

Fired,'" she read. She lowered the paper and looked at what was left of her yard. Her fingers curled into claws, and the newspaper crumpled in her grip. "Fired? Oh, he'll have *much* more than his job to worry about—that coach *and* the brats who did this to me!"

Graham Senior audibly gulped and slowly backed off the porch. A line of sweat formed on his forehead. Alexandra sneered at him.

"Yes, Mr. Herndon, they'll get what's coming to them."

"Best leave it all how it is so the sheriff can see it, Alexandra," Graham Senior croaked nervously. He cowered under the look she shot him.

"Leave it? For the town to see? So everyone can pity a defeated woman? No. No!"

"Pa," the younger Graham said from the sidewalk, "maybe we should get back to the restaurant. Pastries in the oven and all."

"Yes," Graham Senior responded, turning toward his son and rushing back through the destruction. "I'm sorry this happened, Alexandra. Good luck with everything."

"Not a word about this to anyone, Mr. Herndon. You either, boy. Not. One. Word."

The Herndons nodded to her in unison and then hurried back to the diner. Alexandra stood and glared at them until they were out of sight. Then she looked around the garden one more time and went to work cleaning the mess and salvaging what flowers she could. She arranged them into small bouquets that she would sell for cheap that day, then close up her business for the next several weeks until new flowers grew in to replace the mangled ones. But she wouldn't be idle during that time.

No, no, there was much work to be done.

Things to be planned.

Revenge to be had.

Of course, in her rage, she didn't notice the tracks crisscrossing what had once been her neat rows of flowers.

Thin tracks.

Tire tracks.

From a wheelchair, perhaps?

Chapter Ten

"Enough bacon, Shirley! You *do* want to marry a nice young man one of these days, don't you?"

Shirley dropped the crispy pig flesh onto her plate and glared at her mother but didn't speak.

"Now, you best get along to Ms. Butterfield's place. She'll be waiting for you to get her out of bed and dress her."

"If you wanted to take away my appetite, that's all you had to say, Mother," Shirley said. Even though she had spent less than a month as Agnes Butterfield's personal assistant, Shirley had seen more than enough of the bruised and bloated woman. She was scared that Agnes's horrendous personality and general disdain for just about everyone would rub off on her and that she would become an old, lonely grouch herself one day.

Shirley got up from the table and stomped to her room. She felt a little foolish stomping away like a child, but that's what living at home and completely depending on her parents did to her. She loaded a fresh roll of film, checked herself in the mirror, and then rushed down the hall and out the front door before her mother could get in another word or figure out that Shirley had been fired by Ms. Butterfield. She pulled her bike off the porch and sped away.

She needed to head east, but she expected her mother to be looking out the kitchen window, so she rode in the direction of the Raventree Inn. Once Shirley was a block away, she cut through the neighborhood park. The sight of it shocked her; tire tracks tore up the grass, and beer bottles and other trash littered the playground. The varsity football players had struck again, it seemed. It was no different from when she was in high school. The team was out of control every year, and the town seemed content to let it happen as long as those kids kept winning district titles.

Shirley pedaled faster and didn't let up until she was past the outskirts of town. She turned into the abandoned fairgrounds and parked her bicycle behind a lavatory that was locked up for the season. Weeds had grown and dried up in the weeks since the fair had rolled out of town. Shirley regretted not wearing boots; burrs were already sticking to her socks and shoes. The path wasn't nearly as pleasant as when it was covered with grass in the spring. She tried to ignore the annoyance and started up the incline.

The brown turned to green as she neared the crown of the hill and the tall shrubbery that marked the border of the Winfield estate. Shirley knew from her previous walks up here that a black iron fence surrounded the property, hidden behind the bushes. She waved the thick spiderwebs away and squeezed herself through the shrubbery so she could get a good look.

The yard on the other side of the iron bars was breathtaking. Lush lawns looked as if nobody had told them it was the driest part of summer. The rows of flowers would have made Alexandra Pennington blush. The soothing sound of fountains filled the air. Koi ponds dotted the landscape with small wooden bridges spanning portions of the water. Walkways spread out in several directions, lined with pergolas covered in neatly groomed climbing plants. The paths led to statues of Winfield ancestors, benches, or other features. One ended at a large gazebo where Shirley knew Phillip enjoyed taking his meals on nice days, especially when he was with Rebecca Abrams. That was where she looked for him now.

Phillip sat there, just as she had expected, before a bowl of fruit and a covered silver platter that Shirley imagined contained something wonderful— eggs Benedict with delectable hollandaise sauce, perhaps. A glass of orange juice sat next to a teacup on a saucer. What wasn't at the table, she noticed, was the mystery woman. Phillip sat alone, a half-folded newspaper in his hands. Shirley was quite shocked to see that it wasn't even the big city paper but the Raventree Herald. She wished she could tell her father; perhaps he'd appreciate knowing that the wealthiest resident in town was a reader of his paper.

Shirley did what she always did when she made the trek up here; she raised her camera and took a photo of the unaware Phillip Winfield. Just as she prepared to snap another, she noticed movement in her peripheral vision. She turned toward an open French door of the manor, from which the red-haired woman emerged, guided by Phillip's butler, Gerald Weatherby. Phillip stood up at the sight of his guest and waited for her to sit across from him before dropping back into his own seat.

Just like the previous day at the station, there was no particular warmth or affection in the greetings between Phillip and the woman. He smiled politely, but it wasn't at all like the smile Shirley had seen him give Rebecca, one of pure joy, of love, of desire.

Shirley knew that smile well, as it graced several of the photos on her bedroom walls.

She stood and watched them, not able to hear any words, only the very occasional laugh. Their conversation seemed so straightforward and businesslike. At one point, Mr. Weatherby retrieved what appeared to be photo albums or scrapbooks and handed them to the woman. She flipped through pages and pointed out several things, and Phillip just nodded and smiled politely or shook his head. The pair nibbled at their food as they talked. Eventually, the guest stood up, and Mr. Weatherby led her back to the house. The albums still sat on the table, but Phillip didn't seem interested in them. He opened the newspaper again and read up on local news. Perhaps Herman's photographs of the scene at the Mertz house had caught his eye. Maybe she should have accepted Herman's offer and taken the photos for the story.

At least *then* Phillip Winfield might have known that Shirley Bettencourt even existed.

She turned and contorted her way out of the shrubs. The jagged end of one branch sliced into her arm and drew blood. She bit her lip to avoid crying out. She took another step, but her camera strap had caught somewhere in the shrubbery. Shirley yanked at it, and it gave way, along with a few inches of the bush. She lost her balance and rolled several feet down the slope. This time, she failed to stifle her cry of pain. It came out as a scream, as if she were a kettle at full boil. Shirley came to a halt and lay there halfway down the hill, too terrified to let out any more noise.

When she heard footsteps, she didn't need to look up to know who was approaching.

"Miss, are you all right? Here, let me help you up."

Shirley's right hand shot up to her hair and patted down a few loose strands. Her left hand felt around for the camera, which had landed a foot away from her, unbroken. She pulled it close, praying Phillip hadn't taken notice of it.

"I'm sorry to have disturbed you, sir," Shirley said. She turned her head and flashed a bashful smile. She felt her cheeks flame, but she couldn't look away. She noticed him glance down at her camera. "I was taking some shots of the scenery here to document the effects of the annual fair on the fields. I needed a picture from up high to really get the whole scope."

Before she knew it, Phillip had one hand on her left arm, the other on her back. He guided her to her feet.

"It looks like you're in one piece, but I'd feel better if you came up to the house with me. My butler, Mr. Weatherby, is a fine medic. He can dress and bandage any cuts or scrapes. My name is Phillip, by the way."

He put out his right hand. She took it in her own.

Shirley melted at his touch. He was genuinely concerned about her.

"Sh-Shirley Bettencourt," she managed.

Phillip Winfield knows my name, she thought. *And I've made an absolute fool of myself!*

"So, Ms. Bettencourt, what do you say? Will you come for a quick checkup?"

"I must be going, Mr. Winfield."

"Phillip," he said, flashing his perfect teeth.

"I must be going, Phillip, but thank you for your concern. I'm doing just fine—it was only a slight tumble. Have a good day!"

With that, she was off.

SHIRLEY RUSHED BACK TOWARD HOME. SHE HAD originally planned to ride over to the newspaper office to use the darkroom there. That was something her father actually allowed from time to time, as long as it was for her own personal projects and not to get photos into the newspaper.

But then there was Herman Stanley.

I should have invited him along, she thought. *He'll be hurt if he knows I was out there without him. Doubly so if I tell him about Phillip, my rescuer.*

She had created a small personal darkroom space in the basement of her house as well, but her mother was always going down there to nag her about one thing or another. It was just the right time to say she was home on a lunch break, at least.

Shirley wheeled up the driveway and parked her bicycle just inside the back gate. As she lowered the kickstand, her mother's sobbing sounded through the open dining room window. She crept farther up the side yard toward the window, carefully sticking to the stepping stones to avoid crunching on the gravel.

"I just don't know what to do with her," her mother was saying between wet gasps. "If she can't even hold a job with you, what hope does she have? I don't think she even has any prospects for marriage. I don't even know if she likes any of the young men in town!"

A cackle rang out. Shirley knew what miserable lump that laugh came from.

"Now, now," Agnes Butterfield said without a hint of sympathy. "We know that girl of yours is into one boy, at least. The pictures you showed me in her room are proof of that. I say knock her down a peg or two. Burn those pictures and forbid her from spying on Phillip Winfield. She's too old to be having such girlish fantasies. She may as well learn it now."

"I think you're right, Aggie. Speaking of Phillip, is it true about the new woman?"

"It is indeed! She even spent the night at his estate, as far as we know. Spoiling that purity before the wedding, I fear. You see, Susan? It's good Shirley isn't involved in that kind of thing, at least."

Susan Bettencourt let out another sob. Shirley peeked through the window and witnessed Agnes taking a sip of tea, seemingly to stifle a laugh.

"You know, Susan, speaking of illicit love, I just came from Doctor Chou's office. When I had my unfortunate spill last month, Doctor Marshall was out of town, so I had to see Chou instead. Anyway, I believe I smelled the perfume of a certain florist we both know. One of her day-old bouquets was sitting in a vase in the office, and Kenneth Chou had a little more spring in his step than usual. I'm telling you, deary, I think there is something going on between Alexandra Pennington and the young doc."

Mrs. Bettencourt gasped as if this news were the most shocking thing she'd heard in her life. The women continued to gossip while Shirley crept through the back door and into the cellar to develop her film.

Burn those pictures?

Girlish fantasies?

If anything, I'm the most realistic person in this town, Shirley thought. *Something sick plagues Raventree Hollow, and I'll be damned if I let it infect me, too.*

Chapter Eleven

The gong of the bell reverberated in Laurence's ears. His entire body vibrated as if he'd received an electric shock. He wasn't certain, but it felt as if the silver caps over his rotted molars had shaken loose. A ringing in his ears followed, blocking out all other noise.

Laurence sat up in a stupor. He had indulged in some light drinking during his younger years, even in seminary, but he had always been careful to stop before the buzz toed into drunken territory. He imagined being intoxicated might feel something like what he was experiencing now, his head spinning, his memory hazy.

Where am I? Laurence thought. *How did I get here?*

His pupils adjusted to the darkness that engulfed him. To his sides were ancient, dusty brick walls. He sat on a wooden platform, and a staircase descended into darkness below him. He looked up, but the motion caused stars to spin around him. Had he been standing, he would have collapsed from the vertigo. Laurence tried again, tilting his head up more slowly. There, as he had expected, was a massive bell. Ropes protruded from it and traveled down through an opening in the center of the platform, just big enough for Laurence to have fallen through had he rolled over in his sleep moments before.

The bricks.

The bell.

The convent?

How could I possibly be here?

Laurence noticed a gritty feeling under his hands. He lifted them from the wooden platform and rubbed them together. Several morsels of what he thought at first must be sand fell from his sweaty palms. *No, not sand. Termite droppings. This must be some place ancient. It has to be the convent.*

Next to where he sat, the rope swayed slightly. Someone must have moved it, as Laurence didn't feel any wind flowing through the tower. It wasn't enough force to ring the bell, so someone must have brushed against it by accident. Laurence tried to call out, but something was wrong. No air seemed to leave his windpipe. His mouth was dry, his throat scratchy, coarse. He tried to clear it and again felt something gritty. Laurence took a deep breath in but choked. He mustered up just enough saliva to spit onto the floor. In the moonlight that shined through the openings around the bell, Laurence could see his spit on the platform. Had those termite droppings come from inside his throat, or had his spit merely mixed with them on the floor? He noticed movement in the sticky liquid, and he leaned in to see termites crawling around. He wiped away the spittle on his lip, then peered at the back of his hand: another termite. He swatted it with his other hand and jumped to his feet.

He suddenly itched all over. He patted his clothing, his neck, his arms, his legs. It was the first time he noticed what he was wearing. His bedtime flannels hung loosely around his body. His feet were bare, his toes amidst the grit on the dusty, infested platform.

What time is it? The bell was ringing when I awoke, he thought. *Was it just once, or did I sleep through others? No, I couldn't have slept through it. It must be one o'clock in the morning.*

Laurence reached for the handrail and carefully descended the first wooden stair. It trembled and groaned under his weight. Whoever was at the bottom would surely know that he was on his way down. The room spun again as he tried to look into the darkness below. He pulled himself against the brick wall, away from the edge of the stairs. Laurence didn't trust the frail handrail to support his weight should his vertigo sweep him off his feet. He sat on the top step for a few moments to calm himself, and then rose and resumed his descent.

After fourteen or fifteen steps that hugged the rounded walls, he arrived at the next platform. The floor was bare aside from dust and droppings. He continued down the next flight of stairs to an identical empty landing. And then another, and another. Five, then six platforms down, and still there were more stairs.

Laurence sat down, needing to collect his breath and his thoughts. He had seen the convent only from the outside, from down below in town. Sure, it was far away, but it had been there his entire life in Raventree Hollow. He knew the bell tower wasn't more than six stories tall. It couldn't be.

No matter the impossibility of the situation, there was nothing to do but continue on, so that's what he did, down another flight of stairs, this one double the length of the previous stretches between floors. After nearly thirty steps, a smell hit Laurence's nose, like sulfur covering up rot and decay. The scent of death. His eyes watered as his nostrils burned. His sinus cavities seemed to swell, and again his balance faltered. Laurence's right foot missed the next step and came down hard on the one below it. It was a fractured stair, cracked with age and neglect, and it splintered under his unintentional force. A large sliver jabbed into his foot, and without thinking, he leaned against the unstable handrail. As he had feared, the rail couldn't support his weight. It gave way, and he toppled into the darkness.

He fell.

And fell.

He kept falling through the air, unable to scream out in terror. His arms flailed as he tumbled in black nothingness, no windows around him to illuminate his surroundings with moonlight, showing him what he might grab hold of or how far away the bottom was.

The fingers on his left hand made contact with something.

The rope!

Laurence tried and tried again to grab hold of it, but it was just barely out of reach. Another attempt, and his fingers wrapped around it. He quickly grabbed hold with his other hand as well, but he couldn't yet stop his fall. The rope was rough, and it tore into his skin. For a split second, his fall seemed to slow, but the pain was too much, and he involuntarily let go. His free fall continued for a few more seconds before he hit the bottom.

For a moment, it felt no different from hitting concrete. He thought he'd be dead, but the very act of thinking meant that wasn't yet true. Laurence realized he was engulfed in a liquid. Water, perhaps, though it felt too thick to be water. Mucky. There was an unnatural warmth to it, too. It got under his eyelids, and his eyes stung as he tried to keep them closed. It was in his nostrils, seeping into his throat as he plunged down farther from the force of his fall.

He flailed his limbs, but fighting the thick liquid tired him out quickly. Laurence was ready to give in to the pull. He relaxed his body. *The good Lord will take me to His heavenly home now*, he thought.

That was when he saw a face in his mind—a beautiful face that would have made him smile and blush under any other circumstance. *Katrina Givens. She'll never know what happened to me if I die here tonight. I can't die. I can't give up.*

Alertness swept back into his body, and Laurence managed to swim up to the surface. His head broke into the open, and he took a deep breath of the putrid air. As soon as his lungs filled with enough oxygen, he paddled over to the edge and pulled himself up onto a warm brick floor. On his hands and knees, he put his head down and vomited up everything that had entered his body in that unholy place.

"Ugh," he heard himself croak. It was the closest to normal his voice had sounded since he'd woken up in the tower. He tried again. "He... hel... help me!"

His weak call for help echoed throughout the tower above him. He collapsed onto his belly in the pile of vomit, not caring about the mess. He heard something approaching.

Footsteps?

Laurence rolled over, rubbed his eyes, and opened them. In a half circle around him, holding torches, stood seven women, their faces buried in shadows underneath their wimples. They didn't speak. Laurence tried to cry out to them but once again found that no sound would escape his mouth.

A knock broke the silence.

And then another.

Laurence's vision faded under a veil of darkness.

ANOTHER KNOCK SOUNDED OUT.

Laurence opened his eyes to find the veil still covering him. He reached up and pushed it back.

A sheet.

His sheet. He was in his own bed. The morning sunlight shone through the cracks around the curtains. Laurence glanced at the clock. It was five after nine.

There was another knock on the door. It sounded like a lighter touch than what he had heard in that strange place just moments before, but he also knew that the mind played tricks on a dreamer who was deep in the clutches of sleep.

Was that all it was? he thought. *Just a dream?*

Laurence found it easy enough to sit up, but a feeling of vertigo fell over him again for a second or two. It faded as he got to his feet and let out a yelp of pain. He lifted his right leg and inspected the bottom of his foot. Two inches of splintered wood protruded from his flesh. Laurence winced as he pulled it out. He brought it close to his face for a better look, then observed his hands. The flesh on his palms and fingers was missing a layer or two. There was no blood, and the wounds didn't even look very fresh, but they were there, clear as day.

Another knock at the door. *Katrina*, Laurence thought. They had made plans to meet in the square in front of the church at a quarter to nine, and he had overslept. He pulled on his brown bathrobe and hobbled to the door.

The August morning sunlight blinded him momentarily when he opened it, but as soon as his eyes adjusted, he caught sight of the beautiful face he had seen in the deep muck of that tower.

"Katrina," he said, immediately satisfied that his voice had returned to normal.

"Why, Laurence Wolfram, you kept me waiting," she said in jest.

"I'm so sorry," he said, panicking. "I overslept. I was having the strangest dream that I couldn't seem to wake from until you knocked."

"I'm only kidding, my dear friend. It was only a quick jaunt over here from your church." Katrina's smile faltered as she examined Laurence. She reached up and rubbed his cheek. "You don't look so good, Laurence. Do you feel ill?"

"Like I said, strange dreams. It's nothing, honestly. I'd like to forget about it and go on about my day. Say, why don't you give me five minutes to wash up, and then we can go down to Graham's Diner for some breakfast."

"Are you sure?" Katrina took a step into Laurence's apartment, but he moved forward to block her way. He had never invited her in. He didn't feel it would be appropriate, what with him being the pastor of the town's church and her being an unequally yoked pagan woman. It didn't matter whether or not he was madly in love with her. People would get the wrong idea. They would talk. Everyone in town would know by the time he arrived back at the church for his workday later that morning. All it would take was someone like—

"Oh, good morning, Ms. Jennings," Laurence called to his neighbor, who was walking down the hall of the apartment complex at that very moment and gawking at the two of them. All it would take was someone like Ronnie Marie Jennings to get the wrong idea. Laurence pushed the door partway closed, forcing Katrina to step back into the hall. He turned to her again. "Yes, I'll meet you at the diner. I'll just be five minutes. Save us a table."

He closed the door the rest of the way, turned, and leaned against it. He took a deep breath and listened to Katrina's footsteps as she walked away. Once he could no longer hear her, he hurried to the bathroom sink. He splashed his face with water, wiped it dry with a towel, and looked at himself in the mirror. His hair was drenched with sweat, as were his pajamas. The smell emanating from the clothes was wretched. It smelled just like the muck he had fallen into during the dream.

On his way to the diner, it took all of his willpower to avoid looking toward at the hill rising above the west side of town. He didn't need to see it. Deep in his soul, he could *feel* the collective gaze of the Sisters of Mercy behind the fortified walls of their convent, boring a hole right through him.

They were staring.

Judging.

Beckoning.

Chapter Twelve

Days of pleasure and rest didn't come often for Alexandra. Day in and day out, she toiled in that garden of hers. Seven days a week, she planted and picked, weeded and watered, worked the booth, made bouquets, tied ribbons, smiled for customers and passersby. She brought beauty to Main Street with her perfectly placed home and its gorgeous blooms.

So finding Alexandra on a train leaving Raventree Hollow late on a Friday morning was as rare as some of the exotic flowers in her little nursery.

Yet here she was.

On her way to the big city.

This wasn't quite a day of pleasure, though, and certainly not a day of rest. She was here on a particular type of business—the business of revenge.

The August sun shone brightly into the passenger car, but Alexandra's deeds were dark.

She stayed on the train through its stop at the central station. Downtown wasn't quite where she was headed. No, what she needed was on the east side of town. Perhaps there would be time for fancy dress shops and cloth napkin restaurants later.

Alexandra trekked down the cracked pavement of the East Forty-Third Street train station. She pushed her sunglasses up and pulled the brim of her hat a little lower. Clutching her purse tightly between her upper arm and her bosom, she side-eyed all of the passersby on the street. She was walking aimlessly, but she didn't want to *look* like she had no idea where she was headed. This was the side of the big city with a certain reputation. A different class of folk.

This was where she was sure she would find a killer.

A line of motorcycles blocked the sidewalk in front of an establishment with assorted beer signs in the window. It was as good a place as any for Alexandra Pennington to start. She tiptoed between two of the bikes, unsure whether she'd knock them down like a row of dominos if she were to bump one of them. Rambunctious tunes blasted out at her when she opened the door, and she stood dumbfounded in the doorway, trying to adjust to the cave-like dimness of the place. Even once her eyes adjusted, she had to squint through a haze of smoke before she could find her way to the bar.

"Glass of white wine, if you would," she said to the barkeep. The man seemed roughly her age, but perhaps grayer, especially in the rough patches sprouting from his face. His white T-shirt was covered in what she could only assume were beer stains. He took one puff on his hand-rolled cigarette as he stared at her, exhaled through his nose, and turned to the wall of bottles behind him. He returned a few seconds later with a full wineglass. Alexandra had her coin purse out, but the man walked away to collect empty glasses on the other side of the bar.

Alexandra turned around and took in the room. At one end, a group of young men—Alexandra guessed college-age, but not college-bound—were sliding some kind of discs down a long powdered table. They paid her no mind. A quite elderly couple was nestled into a corner booth—a second home to them, from the looks of it—making out like a pair of teenagers after the prom. She blushed at the sight of it. The other tables on that side of the tavern were empty. Turning the other way, she found a booth containing three gentlemen playing cards, another where a man was hunched over asleep on the table, and a couple more where men sat alone, contemplating their cups. At the far side of the bar, a few men sat with bottles in hand and one wrote in a notebook while sipping on a steaming mug of coffee.

Not one of them looked like what she thought she needed.

Alexandra took her wineglass and trotted over to a table in the middle of the room. Between songs on the jukebox, she tried her best to eavesdrop on the surrounding conversations, but to no avail. When she ordered a second glass, she asked the proprietor if he could lower the volume just a tad. He grunted an unintelligible reply, but by the time she returned to her table, she could finally hear some of the other voices in the room.

Money for rent. Card up the sleeve. Don't tell my wife. Lunch break is over, gotta run. Nothing she'd hoped to hear.

She was on her third glass when a man strutted in and approached the bar. A dozen people had come and gone, consuming their liquid lunches and returning to work. This man, however, settled into a booth once he'd received his mug of dark ale. He looked like he was ready for business. Dark business.

Alexandra was a bit shaky on her walk up to order a fourth drink, this time switching to a cheap red. Upon her return to the table, she shifted her chair just enough to get a better view of the newcomer. He flagged down a woman in her late twenties when she walked through the door, and she sat across from him without ordering anything.

Snippets of their conversation wandered over to Alexandra's snooping ears, but she couldn't get a good grasp on what they were talking about.

"Cheating son of a devil," she made out quite clearly from the woman, and "Caught him with his little floozy." The woman passed an envelope to the man, then seemed to cry for a moment before rushing to the exit with her head down.

Alexandra decided to go for it.

She stood up, downed the half glass of wine that remained, and stumbled over to the man's booth. She was tipsier than she'd realized. Perhaps she was making an Agnes Butterfield–size mistake. But it was too late to turn back now.

The man gave a bemused look to the fifty-year-old florist who had joined him in his booth. "Something I can do for you, lady?"

"Why, yes, I think there is," Alexandra said, but then she didn't know how to proceed. The man sat there, looking her over with a smirk on his face. He lit a cigarette before breaking the silence.

"Listen, I don't got all day, lady. What is it you think you want? It's not too late to go back over to your table."

"Don't call me 'lady.' It's patronizing."

"Well, you are a lady, ain't you, lady?"

"Of course I am. But where are my manners? I'm Alexandra Pennington." She reached across the table to shake his hand, but he blew out smoke and reached for his glass instead of taking it.

"Best you don't learn my name, Ms. Pennington. I like to keep it informal, if you know what I mean." He looked around to make sure nobody was watching, perhaps afraid this was a setup, that maybe the cops were on to him. Apparently, he found nothing too worrying. "Listen, maybe you think this is what you want, but I don't think you do. I'm in the business of no returns. No refunds. You catch my drift?"

"I catch it very well," Alexandra said. It came out more coolly that she expected. She let herself smirk a bit.

"You got a cheating old man? Boss been copping a feel up your dress? What is it?"

"Is it always one of those?"

"Pretty much, with you broads. All the same, your type."

"And what type is that?" Alexandra wished she had ordered more wine before coming over here.

"Middle-aged townie broads. Living in delightful houses with their kids and all their pretty things. Fancy hats. Doilies on the tables. That flowery potpourri smell greeting you when you open the front door. Not a struggle in the world. So when a man does you wrong one time, you snap. You're ready to kill him right there, but you can't. So you take that man's money, and you hire another man to come do him in. Is that it?"

"Well, there's a man, all right. But not a boss or a husband. You see—"

"I don't care," he interrupted. "Don't need the story, just the payment and where I can find the target. Two thousand up front."

"Dollars?" Alexandra nearly shouted.

"Keep it down, lady," the man said to her, an unforgiving look crossing his face. "You obviously ain't done your research on this. It ain't a clean and easy thing, doing a hit. Of course it ain't cheap, or you'd be seeing unexplained deaths all over the papers every day. Now, you got the two grand, or am I out of here?"

Alexandra thought about her income, which had dried up entirely for at least a few weeks thanks to that coach and his team. Property taxes were due in a couple of months. Her savings had dwindled throughout the year. There was no way, and the man saw it on her face. He pulled out another cigarette, lit it, and handed it over to Alexandra.

"Sit here with that. Deep breaths. Your problems ain't as bad as they seem, lady. Just walk away from whatever your issue is. Trust me on this." The man scooted out of the booth and walked out the door.

Before the cigarette had burned down too close

to her fingers, the man she had seen at the bar with a notebook and coffee plopped down into the recently vacated seat in the booth. He looked around with a bit of a self-satisfied smile on his face.

"I can't believe I'm sitting here," he said under his breath.

"Excuse me?" Alexandra said.

She took in the appearance of the man across from her. He was short, perhaps five and a half feet, and a bit plump. He was balding. Little round glasses circled his eyes. His hands seemed quite soft. Not the kind of man Alexandra would have expected to see in such an establishment, though she was quite out of place herself.

"I'm sorry, let me introduce myself. I'm... well, you can call me Bard." He looked at her as if expecting something. She didn't give it. "Um, sorry. I overheard what you were saying to Wilkinson. I know he didn't accept the, um, job you were trying to give him. So sorry about that. But perhaps I can be of service to you instead?"

"Mr. Bard, I'm not sure I understand. Are you a—"

"Hit man." Bard looked pleased with himself as he uttered the words, even though they sounded quite odd coming from his mouth. He picked up a napkin off the table and dabbed his sweating pate. "Sorry for interrupting you, madam. Yes, I am one of those. Or at least I'm looking to be. This would be my first case. And I'll charge you as such. How does two hundred and fifty sound?"

Alexandra smiled. Perhaps it was all the wine, or maybe there was some natural high from engaging in such deeds, like the way she felt during her secret escapades with the good Doctor Chou. Either way, she felt quite good. She reached her hand across the table, this time knowing it would be met with a shake.

"Make it two hundred, and you've got yourself a job."

THE EFFECTS OF THE ALCOHOL WORE OFF AS Alexandra Pennington took a late afternoon stroll through the Japanese Gardens in the middle of the city. It was a place she remembered visiting a couple of times on dates when she was still a desirous young woman, in the days when life still had so much potential. When her youthful body offered hope of a family. When her laugh was less tainted with weariness. Perhaps it was the beauty of the place that had helped her come to terms with taking over her parents' business in the dead-end town of Raventree Hollow even though she wanted more than anything in the world to study art and antiquities in the big city.

Is it that the alcohol is wearing off? she wondered. *Or is it something else? Being away from Raventree Hollow?* She hadn't noticed anything changing within her on the train into the city, nor had she been in a positive frame of mind at the bar that afternoon, but now several hours away from her hometown felt unexpectedly wonderful to Alexandra. It was as if some insidious entity had wrapped its tentacles around her that first morning she had discovered the eggs and toilet paper. Something evil had injected her with pure anger and despair. She hadn't been herself in several days. In the gardens of the big city, however, the veil of darkness lifted.

And now that she was sober, she had other issues to come to terms with. Issues that the peonies and water irises and camellias wouldn't be able to cover up.

She sat on a bench and looked at the pond before her. What was left in life to look forward to? She was too old to have children. The flowers in her garden would grow back and provide her with a modest income for as long as she continued to keep it up, but even being right on Main Street every day, she was lonely. She felt like she was on the outside of the inner circle of gossip. She had to pass up too many luncheons and teatimes with the other women because she was stuck in her booth, preparing bouquets for their husbands to pick up for them.

There *was* Kenneth. He had professed his love for her just the other night, though it was in the throes of passion. Had he meant it? Was she prepared for the scandal that would surely arise if people found out about them? It wasn't just that he was Chinese American; there was also the issue of age. The good doctor was fifteen years her junior.

But oh, he loved her just right. And she knew she loved him, even if she hadn't felt such a thing in years before he came along.

So what if the coach turned a blind eye while his team played some pranks on the town?

So what if her flowers were ruined? It was nearly autumn, anyway. The weather would soon change, and she would plant the fall breeds in her garden.

There *was* more to live for, gossip be damned.

But there was one problem. She had already set everything in motion. The coach was now the target of that strange little man. Bart? Bard? Whatever throwaway name he had given. And then Alexandra remembered something. She reached into her purse and pulled out a slip of paper the man had torn out of his little notebook. It had his phone number on it. He had asked her to burn it after the job was done— "You'll know when it's done," he had said—and to never contact him again unless there was a very good reason.

Regret was as good a reason as any.

Alexandra rushed out of the garden, crossed the park, and entered one of the many identical corner diners that littered big cities like this one. One of the two phone booths was available, so Alexandra entered it, pulled the door shut, and jammed in a coin. She gave the number to the operator and was connected to a line that rang.

And rang.

And rang.

She fretted all the way back to Raventree Hollow on the train. Her only solace was that it was a small enough town that she'd likely see Mr. Bard before he took action. Visitors were rare enough, and the funny little man would stand out quite a lot.

Or so she hoped.

Chapter Thirteen

*Bless the Lord, O my soul: and all that is within me,
bless His holy name.*

 *Bless the Lord, O my soul, and forget not all
His benefits:*

 *Who forgiveth all thine iniquities; who healeth all thy
diseases;*

 *Who redeemeth thy life from destruction; who crowneth
thee with loving kindness and tender mercies;*

 *Who satisfieth thy mouth with good things; so that thy
youth is renewed like the eagle's.*

And boy, was Pastor Laurence renewed.

As he read Psalm 103 to a full house, he was practically floating off the dais with the Holy Spirit.

A full house. In Raventree Community Church. For the first time in years.

He was sure to bring the fire with his sermon. His

every word seemed to capture the hearts of everybody in the pews. He led the congregation through songs, and Mrs. Eckleman pounded the ivories with more intensity and emotion than he could ever remember hearing from the elderly woman.

As he gave communion near the end of the service, he locked eyes knowingly with every member of Agnes's little gossip group, like members of a secret society sharing in their conspiracy. Every member had brought their family and their neighbors and their friends. Every member, that is, except for Katrina Givens, who was not present.

The impromptu potluck luncheon on the town square afterward felt just like days of old. It was as if the church of his youth had resurrected from the tomb after three very long days.

Pastor Laurence was on top of the world.

"You should have seen it, Kat," Laurence said as they took an evening stroll up and down Main Street through the thick, late summer humidity. "Practically the whole town was there, hungry for the word of God. Singing along to the hymns. Partaking in communion. Fellowshipping with the rest of the congregation afterward. It was incredible! It was—"

"A sham," Katrina interrupted. "It was all built on something quite unholy, Larry, and you know it."

"I'm just doing what you suggested, though! Spending more time with them to draw them back into the church. Exactly what you wanted me to do."

"And I was wrong, Larry. I know that now. It just does not feel right. And something with *you* doesn't feel right, either."

It wasn't the first time she'd said something like that to Laurence. In their senior year of high school, they had grown very close. They had gone to the prom together and had a wonderful time. Afterward, they had driven a few miles outside of town and up to Kissers' Crest, as the kids had called it back then. Laurence hadn't taken her there with sinful intentions—at least none that he was willing to admit.

They had sat in the car he'd borrowed from his father and looked out at the lights of the town in the distance and up at the stars in the sky. They had chatted, Katrina laughing about Laurence's dancing, Laurence raving about Katrina's beauty. And then talk had turned to the future, as it always does during those adolescent interactions. Laurence had gone on and on about how he wanted to get out of town. How he needed to escape. How it felt like the town had a hold on every person there, and he would break whatever curse was keeping them in that place. He had called Raventree Hollow a parasite, sucking the life from everybody. It had made Katrina sad to see such darkness in her friend. She was to stay and become one of those parasite-infected, mindless prisoners while he was off at seminary. The negativity he had exuded had been out of character for the boy she loved, and she had told him how much it broke her heart to hear him like that.

"I'm in the right frame of mind right now, Kat, more than I've ever been," he said now, but he knew she was spot-on. Now, just like then. He had realized it back then, too, once he'd gone away for his education. He had missed the quaintness and the familiarity and the eccentricities of Raventree Hollow. He had missed *her* most of all. It was as if a veil of darkness had been pulled away from him once he was out of town and he was only able to remember the good parts of his life there. And those good parts had drawn him right back in.

"Look, Kat, you're right. Of course you're right that engaging in their little rumor mill means I'm sinning along with the rest of them. I'll own that. For the word of God says it—*whoso privily slandereth his neighbor, him will I cut off: him that hath an high look and a proud heart will not I suffer.* But if my presence at the three meetings we've attended has drawn them back into the church, is it really so bad?"

"It's all built on lies, so I'd say it *is* pretty bad."

Katrina stopped in her tracks, grabbed Laurence

by the shoulders, and kissed him. Not a sisterly peck on the cheek, but a proper kiss. Then, before he could react, she crossed the street and hurried home. A few passersby stared at Laurence, but he pretended not to notice. There was no use hiding it. Word would spread across town by sunrise.

Sweat dripped down his forehead, but it didn't matter. The sky opened up and washed it all away.

Laurence rushed back to the church through the warm, pouring rain for his evening prayer session.

THE OFFERINGS WERE COUNTED IN THE DIM OFFICE behind the sanctuary. There would be enough funds to cover the church's utilities and other bills, as well as the meager salary Laurence was supposed to be earning. Christmas and Easter services were the only other times this past year that he'd been able to say such a thing. The business he had been engaging in may have been bad—he had come to terms with what Kat had said—but God was good.

Laurence locked the cash and checks in the safe beside his desk and then left the office. The business —the part of his job he loathed—was done. He paced around the church, praying over all the corners of the sanctuary, the pews, the piano, the dais. He prayed for each and every one of the townspeople who had congregated there earlier in the day. He praised the Lord for the work He had done, for the way He had used Laurence. Then he dropped to his knees in front of the cross and begged for the Lord's forgiveness for his kiss with Kat, for the part he had played in the town's slanderous activities.

"Set a watch, O Lord, before my mouth; keep the door of my lips," he prayed, and then a knock came upon the locked front door of the church. For a moment, he wondered if it was just thunder. Maybe God Himself was sending a sign to Laurence that it was time to change his ways, that Katrina was right. Perhaps the storm had come to cleanse him. But then the knock sounded again.

Laurence stood up and walked out to the narthex. He flipped the light switch, and the fixture overhead flashed before the bulb burned out. *At least I can afford new bulbs this week*, he thought. He proceeded to the door in the dark.

The knocking ceased the moment he touched the knob. He swung the door open to find a most unexpected visitor.

The impossibly ancient woman refused to enter the church, so they stood together on the covered porch despite the rain that whipped through with the evening breeze.

They talked. Or rather, *she* talked while Laurence listened with both awe and fear. He nodded and let out some dumb *yes ma'ams*, *no ma'ams*, and *thank yous* here and there, the best he could do. It was pathetic for a man who used his voice as a big part of his vocation, but there were times to speak, and there were times to listen. This was undoubtedly the latter.

When she finished what she had to say, she turned around without a parting pleasantry and disappeared into the darkness that enveloped the town square.

A jagged bolt of lightning cracked the night sky, permitting Laurence to make out not just the woman's silhouette but the shapes of a dozen others who had apparently been waiting out there amid the stormy blackness.

Laurence waited at the open door for the rumble of the thunder, but it was the ring of his office phone that broke the atmospheric silence. He closed and bolted the door, ran through the sanctuary, and entered his office.

Kat, you know just how to time things, he thought as he picked up the receiver.

"Hello?"

The voice on the other end was as unexpected as his visitor.

"Mr. Winfield! No, it's not a bad time; I was just locking up the church for the night."

Chapter Fourteen

"Y"ou'll never guess it this time," Ronnie Marie Jennings blurted out as she pushed through the front door of the Raventree Inn. "Two things, in fact!"

Ronnie Marie had been pounding on the door for the several minutes it took for Agnes Butterfield to pull herself out of bed, cover up with a robe, and hobble to her wheelchair. Agnes was still camping out on a twin bed on the first floor in the room that once served as the inn's business office, back when there was actually business to be had. She'd grumbled all the way to the door, unlocked the bolt, and nearly tipped backward in her chair as the door flew open.

"I don't care if it's Jimmy Stewart declaring his undying affection and proposing marriage to me in the middle of his latest picture. If you wake me up this early again, I'm going to poison your tea so that your guts seep straight out of—"

"Oh, Aggie, you're such a dear," Ronnie Marie said. She stepped around the wheelchair and pushed Agnes toward the kitchen. "You're really going to want to hear this. I just came back from the city, as I always do on Monday mornings. Weekends with Mother usually drain me, but that train couldn't come soon enough this time so I could get to you."

"If I had known it was *you* professing your undying love for me, I definitely would not have gotten out of bed just now."

"Hilarious, Ag," Ronnie Marie said as she fired up the burner under the kettle and got the loose-leaf tea ready to steep. "When you're ready to listen, I'm all ready to dish, and you are honestly going to die when you hear this."

"Put on the pot of oatmeal, and then I'll listen to you blab about whatever you want."

There was a noticeable lack of good humor in Agnes's voice, as always. The folks of Raventree Hollow regularly speculated about why Ronnie Marie put up with the old wench. The leading rumor was that Ronnie Marie had been one of Herbert Butterfield's many mistresses over the years, and she felt so guilty over Herbert abandoning Agnes with the failing inn that she went out of her way to make Agnes feel loved. Others believed—and rightly so—that Ronnie Marie was so accustomed to abusive old women like her own mother that Agnes felt just like family to her. Either way, everyone thought Ronnie Marie was far too accommodating of Agnes.

Ronnie Marie set the table and laid out two bowls of oatmeal, freshly sliced bananas and strawberries, sugar, honey, and tea. Her voice echoed around the inn's oversize dining hall as Agnes pulled up to the table in her wheelchair.

"You see, Mother was quite irritable all morning yesterday. I tried and tried to cheer her up, but nothing was working. So I crushed up two of her evening sleeping pills and mixed them into her soup during luncheon. Once she was out cold, I decided to treat myself for my birthday."

"Your birthday was yesterday?"

"It was indeed."

"Oh." No *happy birthday* from Agnes—no surprise there. "Go on with it. I may not have all day if a customer comes to stay." She hadn't had a customer since June, and today was unlikely to be any different, but Ronnie Marie wasn't fazed by any of it.

"Yes, of course. I should back up, actually. Before I even ventured to the city to visit Mother on Friday, two things happened. First, as I was leaving my apartment around nine in the morning, do you know who I saw?"

"Both Presidents Roosevelt holding hands in the stairwell?"

"Very funny, Agnes. No, even better: the good pastor in his pajamas and his witchy lover, leaving his apartment after what must have been a very lustful night together. He looked like he was covered in sweat!"

"Our own Pastor Laurence? You don't say!" The anger seemed to dissipate from Agnes and float off with the steam coming from her tea. Her devious smile flashed, showing a mouthful of half-chewed oats. "He did seem to have quite a spring in his step during Sunday morning's service. Katrina wasn't there, though. She must want to keep it a secret."

"Imagine the scandal if the congregation should hear of it! I mean, we've all been whispering about the two of them for years. Decades, really. So it's not too much of a surprise, but to finally have confirmation after all this time!"

"What else did you see on Friday?"

"After that incredible encounter in the apartment building, I made my way to the train, and guess who else was riding to the city?"

"The hell if I know, Ronnie Marie. How many men in Raventree Hollow commute to their cushy jobs in the big city every day? You want me to name every one of them?"

"This wasn't one of those men. It was our good friend Alexandra Pennington."

"Well, I guess that does make sense after what I—um, after what was done to her garden. She didn't have anything left to sell in her little stall by Friday. Must have gone to get new plants or something."

"She had quite a look on her face, Agnes. I was a bit scared of her, to tell the truth. She didn't even buy her fare for downtown, as I would have expected. She was going a little farther down the line. I don't know any nurseries on the east side of the city."

Agnes contemplated the second bit of news for another moment. "I'll see if I can find out more from her later," Agnes said. "Maybe she's taken on another lover out there, if Doctor Chou isn't enough for her."

Ronnie Marie sipped her tea, and when she pulled the cup away from her lips, Agnes caught a devious smile on the woman's face.

"You still have something enormous to tell, don't you, girl? What a productive weekend this was for you. I'm all ears, Ronnie."

"Well, if you're ready for this one, I suppose I'll tell it! After I knocked out Mother with those pills, I walked downtown to a steak house I've often passed but never entered. I was ready to treat myself. It was quite crowded in there, so I agreed to take a seat at the bar. Two seats down from me was someone *quite* special. I didn't even know they were admitted into restaurants like that, but I suppose the big city is quite a progressive place."

"You don't mean—"

"Rebecca Abrams. Alive and well. And get this: still very much engaged to Phillip Winfield."

Ronnie Marie paused for Agnes's reaction. The eternal grouch held her spoon halfway to her mouth, the liquid from her oatmeal running like a waterfall into her lap. Agnes didn't appear to notice her own mess. A range of emotions cycled quite visibly over her wretched face. Ronnie Marie didn't dare interrupt her.

Agnes set the spoon down and rolled away from the table. She parked herself in front of the large window overlooking what had once been a vegetable and herb garden, back when she had a chef on staff who grew some of the food that was served to patrons of the inn. The abandoned soil was a muddy mess, churning under the heavy drops of rain. The worms and snails were undoubtedly having a feast in the soft ground, consuming the rot and decay to their hearts' content.

I've staked my reputation on this, Agnes thought. *I've got half the town involved in this piece of gossip. They haven't thought twice about my injury or my drinking since last week. And now I hear that Winfield is still engaged to that hussy?*

"There's one more thing," Ronnie Marie said. Agnes broke out of her daze. "It seems she was on a trip around the world with some friends and wasn't due back for another week. She was too lovesick, though, and returned early. She's coming to Raventree Hollow on the afternoon train to surprise Phillip."

Agnes turned her chair to face Ronnie Marie. Even though she had seen wickedness in Agnes many times before, there was something especially nefarious in the look her friend was giving her now.

"Surprise, you say? So Phillip doesn't know she's coming?" Agnes cackled and rolled off toward the hallway. "Perhaps things aren't as dire as I thought. This sounds like a situation I can control."

"Wait, where are you going, Aggie?"

"I'm getting dressed, and then I'm going to go see someone."

"Who?"

Agnes turned around as her friend caught up in the hall. She reached up to Ronnie Marie's face and patted the woman's cheeks as if she were a child.

"Our little lover boy. Thanks to you, we have collateral."

"Phillip Winfield?"

"No, you idiot. Not him."

Perhaps she should have called first. The doors of the church were closed. Agnes didn't dare attempt to rise from her wheelchair and climb the steps in the rain. She rolled around to the side of the church, where a ramp led to an alternate entrance, but as she expected, it was also locked. She huddled under the overhang to catch some relief from the rain and knocked on the door.

If only that no-good Ronnie Marie had come with me, she thought. Ronnie Marie had feigned a cough on the way over and left Agnes on the far side of the town square, claiming she needed to go home and nap off an oncoming head cold.

"Oh, Laurence, open up! It's your dear friend Agnes!"

Still no answer. *Perhaps the good pastor is rolling around in his sheets with his little Katrina*, she thought.

"Ms. Butterfield?" A voice called out. "To what do I owe the pleasure of your company?"

Agnes turned to find Pastor Laurence rushing along the pathway toward the ramp. He wisely held an umbrella. Agnes had been in too much of a rush leaving home to find hers.

"Why, the good Lord's good man. How are you this morning, Pastor Laurence? A late start for you, no?" She backed away from the door enough to allow Laurence to unlock and open it.

"Indeed. I was up late last night," Laurence answered as he guided Agnes's wheelchair into the sanctuary.

"Business, my dear? Or pleasure?" She checked his face for a blush, but he kept his composure.

"Just business. It was quite a busy day with the church being so full and all. Between counting the offerings, praying over the congregation, and receiving a couple of late callers, it was the most productive time I can remember."

"Well, I hope you *do* take the time to take care of your own needs as well." She waited, but there was still no reaction. She decided it was time to go for it. "Anyway, let's be real. I know about you and your little lady friend. Unequally yoked. Unmarried. *Ungodly*."

"Why, Ms. Butterfield, what are you implying?"

"Oh, it's okay, my dear. We all have needs. Carnal needs. Physical needs. Affection. Lust. I get it—I really do. I'm not sure the rest of your flock would be quite so understanding about it, though. Nor about your other extracurricular activities, how you're using our little group to grow your church's attendance. Don't think I don't know what you're doing."

"Now, you're quite out of line, Agnes. I don't

believe you understand everything as well as you think you do."

"Is that so? Because I know all the secrets in this little town. The Winfield family may be the financial royalty around here, but I've got the monopoly on information. On people. The whispers. The jealousy. The hatred. The cheaters and secret lovers. Nothing gets past me, Laurence. But that doesn't mean the information has to spread. The only other person who knows is your neighbor, Ronnie Marie Jennings, and she won't make a peep unless I give her the go-ahead."

She watched as Laurence walked to the back of the sanctuary to turn on the lights. Agnes expected to see fear in his gait, but he appeared quite in control. *There's no way he is immune to this*, she thought.

"While I don't feel the need to defend my personal life to you," Laurence said as he walked back and sat on the pew next to the wheelchair, "I will admit that you are quite right about my participation in your gossip group. My reasons for being there have been anything but pure. I will apologize for my wrongdoings in front of the congregation this Sunday."

"Oh, but Pastor Laurence, it isn't that simple. You *can't* walk away now, not when the story is just getting juicy. We must continue to work together. I have a job that only you can do."

"And what would this job be?"

"You see, breakups are never easy. Sometimes a spurned ex-girlfriend wants to come back into the picture just when the man in question is getting ready to move on with his life. Sometimes this may even happen to fine folks like Phillip Winfield."

"Are you saying Rebecca Abrams is back in town?" Laurence leaned forward. *I've got him right where I want him*, Agnes thought.

"She's arriving this afternoon. She intends to ruin things between Mr. Winfield and his beautiful new lover and stop their eventual wedding. Now, I know you believe in true love, Pastor Laurence. I know you are willing to fight for the sanctity of marriage. That is why I need you for this."

She thought she saw a look of ridicule on Pastor Laurence's face. A smirk, perhaps, but a brief one. She didn't like it.

"You want me to stop her from reaching the manor when she gets to town?" Laurence asked.

"Indeed I do. Tell her you'll give her a ride, that you wouldn't dream of leaving a lady in this pouring rain to wait for the town's only taxicab to arrive at the station."

"What makes you think she'll get in the car with me?"

"She'll trust you of all people, Pastor. You can count on it. I know how to read people. It's my God-given talent, if you will. She'll get in the car with you, and then you will drive her over to my place."

"Why the inn?"

"Let's be frank, Laurence. I won't have any guests. The hospitality business in this town has been dead for months. I'll make up one of the rooms and lock her in. Once the wedding is over with, we will let her go. She'll come to understand it was for her own good, and for Phillip's."

Laurence looked away from her and stared at the cross. Agnes knew the look of a man plotting something, and that was what she saw in his face.

"Well, Pastor?"

He turned back to her with a smile.

"I have another idea. I'm going to take her up the hill."

"You're going to take her right to Phillip Winfield?"

"No, the other hill. To the convent. They'll keep her locked away there, where nobody can hear her scream for help."

"And why would those old nuns help with a deed of this sort?"

His look frightened her.

"Oh, they will, Ms. Butterfield. I have a special connection with them. They'll help me."

Agnes wheeled back away from him. She didn't quite understand the expression on his face. She hadn't expected him to be so willing to go through with her kidnapping plot.

It scared her. She knew she should be pleased that he had agreed to participate, but something seemed off to her. The darkness deep within her screamed at her not to trust the man. He was deceitful.

As if he could read her thoughts, his smile widened. Agnes trembled.

Chapter Fifteen

"Keep me apprised of the situation, Pastor," Agnes Butterfield's voice called across the sanctuary.

Shirley Bettencourt sprinted down the ramp at the side of the church, where she had been listening in on some quite nefarious scheming through the open door. She dove between a metal trash can and an overgrown shrub just ten feet down the alley. The scrape on her knee was only a minor annoyance. It was the mud caking her dress that really bothered Shirley as she hid and listened to the wheelchair squeaking out of the alley and back toward Main Street.

She started to get up when she spotted Pastor Laurence stepping out onto the ramp to watch Agnes wheel away. After a minute, he reentered the church and pulled the side door shut behind him. Shirley ran down the alley toward the access road where her bicycle was leaning against a tree.

She headed three blocks away to Palmdale Avenue, where she'd heard there had been an automobile accident. As she expected, Herman Stanley was circling the scene with his camera, clicking away. Gerald Browning's Studebaker had mounted the back bumper of Caroline Frederick's Chevrolet like two dogs ready to make puppies.

"Why, hiya, Shirl!" Herman called out, pulling back the hood of his rubbery yellow raincoat. Sheriff Holman, Mr. Browning, and Ms. Frederick all turned away from the mess of cars to look at the new arrival but quickly shrugged off Shirley's presence and continued to argue about the damages.

"I knew I'd find you here," Shirley said. She also knew that her appearance would make Herman forget all about his task of reporting on the accident for the paper, but there were more important things going on than a stupid fender bender. "Herman, there is something very iniquitous happening, and I just have to tell someone about it."

"Well, gee, I'm glad you came to me first!" Herman beamed like a middle school girl asked out on her first date by her dream boy. "What is it that has you so troubled?"

Shirley glanced over at the sheriff and the others. Ms. Frederick was shaking with anger and screaming at Mr. Browning, who removed his bowler hat, threw it to the ground, and stomped on it. Folks in the neighboring houses looked on with excitement.

"Let's get out of here, Herman. I'll tell you on the way."

Herman mounted his bicycle, set his camera in the basket under the protection of a canvas sack, and rode off with Shirley.

They pedaled through the rain across Main Street and up to the park in Shirley's neighborhood. The gazebo in the center was empty, so they pulled their bikes up the one step and took cover.

"Take this," Herman said as he peeled off his raincoat. "It's really coming down today, but at least we still have that August heat!"

"Just for a few minutes while I regain feeling in my arms. I don't know what I was thinking, leaving home without a jacket."

"What's on your mind?" Herman asked. He shivered without the raincoat despite his praise of the late summer heat. He was so thin and frail that it didn't surprise Shirley.

She leaned against one of the waist-high rails of the gazebo and surveyed the park. The town kept up the place throughout the year, mowing the grass weekly. Patches of flowers grew at evenly spaced intervals, all donated by Alexandra Pennington, who operated the flower stand on Main Street. Narrow cement sidewalks separated the alternating rectangles of grass and flowers. A wooden playground was lovingly maintained by parents, including Shirley's own father, who had helped install the large slide and the swing set years ago. The gazebo under which she stood played host to a local jazz quartet that performed on Friday evenings when the weather was right.

And yet it all seemed a bit gloomy in the rain. The water brought the worms and beetles out of the ground. The fertile soil in the flower beds had turned to mud, which flowed out onto the sidewalk. Most disturbingly, nobody had come to clean up the mess left by the football team during their raucous night of vandalism the previous week. Toilet paper and trash bloated in the rain. Discarded beer bottles pinged like little drums as the raindrops pegged them. One swing hung lifelessly by one chain, the other side ripped right off.

"Look how it's all coming apart before our eyes, Herman."

"What are you talking about?" Herman put a hesitant hand on her right shoulder, then quickly removed it.

"The park has fallen into disrepair in such a short time. It's normally so beautiful, just as it has always been since we were kids. And now look at it. Folks don't care enough to come clean it up or repair the damage."

"Ah, Shirl, the weather has just been bad, that's all. They'll take care of it when the sun is back out."

"It's not just the park, though. It's this whole town. Something has taken over here, something evil. It has a hold on so many people."

"Did something happen to you, Shirley?"

"To me? No." Shirley turned away from the park and faced Herman. "But something is about to happen to someone else. And one of the few people I would have trusted to put a stop to it is the one who is doing it."

"One of your parents?"

"Pastor Laurence. He's in it deep with Agnes. I overheard them plotting to kidnap Rebecca Abrams on her way into town today."

"He would never!" Herman laughed nervously, but his phony attempt at a smile fell quickly when he saw Shirley was not joking. "I mean, he's always been above the gossip in this town. It was weird that you saw him at that meeting at Agnes's place last week, but I didn't think he was really getting involved."

"It's happening later today! I can prove it if you come with me to the train station. That's where he's planning on abducting Rebecca."

"You have to go to the sheriff about this, Shirley!

Let's ride back to the scene of the accident. He's probably still there."

Shirley turned away and stared at the swings. She'd had many daydreams about sitting on one swing with Phillip Winfield on the other, holding hands as they swayed back and forth in the breeze. Together. Lovers.

"Lovers," she said under her breath.

"What was that?" Herman asked.

Shirley walked over to her bike and mounted it. "I've got to go, Herman. There's someone I need to talk to. I think she's the only one who can talk some sense into Pastor Laurence."

Shirley rode off, Herman's yellow jacket flapping around her body in the wind.

Katrina Givens operated her shop out of a converted garage several blocks away from the business district of Main Street. Her small home sat fifty feet behind the detached garage, which was right on the street. The garage door had long since been replaced with a large front window and a swinging glass door. While the location wasn't ideal for foot traffic, Katrina had managed to stay afloat for several years because of her loyal clientele. Her customers were primarily housewives who waited until their husbands were at work before sneaking off in the family automobiles to purchase Kat's specially prepared herbal teas, home-distilled essential oils, exotic herbs and spices, and alternative medicines. There was nothing unnatural or evil about Katrina, despite what the townspeople enjoyed whispering. No crystal balls or flying brooms or steaming cauldrons full of frog legs and sacrificed virgins.

Shirley was panting when she arrived. The rain still hadn't let up, but someone had apparently forgotten to tell the heat that it should simmer down. She pushed her bike behind some bushes at the side of the shop; the last thing Shirley needed was someone telling her mother she had been with "the witch." She had seen the little dropper bottles tucked behind her mother's sewing supplies in the linen closet—bottles with Katrina's cat stamp and handwriting on the label—but there was no chance of Susan Bettencourt ever owning up to those.

A pair of bells rang out as Shirley pulled the front door open.

"Shirley Bettencourt! It is so nice to see you here!"

Shirley looked around. There was nobody in the shop except Katrina, who was standing behind a counter and mixing up some sort of elixir. She was wearing a baby-blue apron over her pretty yellow dress. Not exactly something a witch would walk around in, if the old fairy tales had any truth to them.

"Hello, Ms. Givens," Shirley said. She took one step inside and allowed the door to glide closed behind her.

"Please, call me Kat. Come on in where it's dry. Can you believe that rain?" Shirley just stood there, as if she was afraid to step farther into the shop. "Shirley, it looks like something is troubling you."

"I'm..." Tears began streaming down her face. "I'm sorry. I shouldn't have come here."

"If you came all this way in that rain, there must be a reason for it." Katrina set down the ingredients she was working with and carefully inserted a stopper into the bottle she was filling. She stepped out from behind the counter and gestured toward a leather love seat along the right wall of the shop. "Please, sit down and let's talk. I promise I'm not as scary as the people in town like to pretend I am."

Shirley heard genuine concern in the woman's voice. She nodded and sat on the leather couch, dripping raincoat and all.

"Would you like some tea, Shirley?"

"That would be nice, thank you."

Katrina inserted infusers filled with some sort of loose-leaf tea into two cups on saucers, then filled them from a kettle on a hot plate behind the counter. She handed one saucer to Shirley as she sat beside the girl. Shirley took a sip, and the mix of spices and herbs made her feel a bit calmer.

"It's Assam tea mixed with my proprietary blend of spices. It's imported from India. You won't see it served anywhere else in this culture-deprived town, I'm afraid."

Shirley laughed at that. She had never actually talked to the woman, even though she'd seen her around town her whole life. She'd always known she'd like Katrina, though. There was an honest warmth to her, and she never seemed to participate in the rumor mill that was so pervasive among the other adults. Her individuality had always inspired Shirley.

"I like it, I really do."

"Good. I'll send some home with you. No charge this time. If I get you hooked now, maybe I'll have another customer for life." Katrina winked at her. "Now, why did you come here? Certainly it wasn't just for a friendly visit, although I wouldn't be sad if it was!"

"Well, it seems silly, really, now that I'm here. But I suppose you're the best person to talk to about this. I know you're very close with Pastor Laurence Wolfram, and I know you were at that meeting at Agnes Butterfield's inn last week."

"Ugh, that woman!" Katrina set her teacup down on the saucer. "Please, allow me to explain my presence there."

"Oh, it's okay. I'm not judging you, Kat."

"I deserve to be judged for being there! Really. It was a dumb move that I normally wouldn't have made. You see, Larry—Pastor Laurence, that is—has been having trouble drawing people into the church. I made a horrible suggestion that he should spend more time with the community in order to make people feel comfortable about spending Sundays there."

"That's not a horrible idea at all."

"Well, not on its own, no. But if I had known ahead of time that we would end up at Agnes Butterfield's, I would have kept my mouth shut. I was just happy to see the spark in Larry's eyes."

"Does he really believe the rumors they're spreading about Phillip Winfield?" Shirley asked.

Katrina stood up and walked to the counter, where she set her tea down. She kept her back to Shirley as if to hide her shame.

"I'm afraid he's very much into it at this point. I tried to talk to him last night, but he was just so ecstatic about how many townsfolk had showed up to the service. He wouldn't hear anything I was saying."

"Katrina, I'm afraid they're going to do something terrible," Shirley said.

Kat turned around at this, looking doubtful. "It was very foolish of Laurence and me to take part in those meetings, but I know there are lines he won't cross. He is a man of his god, after all. He has his church to keep him accountable."

"I was at his church just a few minutes ago. He was inside with Agnes. I overheard what they spoke about, and I think you'll be quite shocked."

"Oh, Shirley, I'm sure it isn't what you thought you heard." But Shirley was quite certain there was doubt on the woman's face.

"I'm not wrong about this. They're going to kidnap Rebecca Abrams in order to keep whatever power they think they've gained with their lies and rumors."

"Kidnap? There is no way, Shirley. I'm sorry, but that just can't be true. Not Laurence. He would never resort to something like kidnapping to further his church. It just makes no sense. You're still so young. Your imagination is still as vivid as your view of the world is naïve."

A vibration sounded. Shirley looked down and realized it was her teacup rattling on the saucer as her hand shook in anger. She set the saucer and cup onto the vacant cushion next to her and stood up.

"Thank you for the tea, Ms. Givens. I'm sorry to have disturbed you."

Without a further farewell or a parting glance, Shirley rushed out the door and retrieved her bike. As she sped down the street, she heard Katrina calling her name, begging her to come back and talk some more.

Shirley ignored the woman. If nobody was going to help her, Shirley would have to take matters into her own hands.

Alone.

Chapter Sixteen

The rain wasn't letting up, and there was still plenty of time until the afternoon train arrived, so Shirley reluctantly pedaled through the downpour toward home.

"Where did you get that hideously oversize raincoat?"

Shirley was shocked out of her daze by the sound of her mother's voice as she stepped through the front door. Susan had apparently been waiting for her daughter's return. She was planted on the couch in the living room just to the left of the front door.

Shirley stared down at the dripping yellow rubber garment she had forgotten she was wearing.

"It belongs to a friend. I forgot my jacket this morning." She started to strip the coat off like a banana peel.

"You forgot your jacket in a storm like this? What were you thinking about instead of using the logic I know you're capable of, Shirley? Or should I ask, *who* were you thinking about?"

"I—"

"Phillip Winfield, perhaps?" Susan gestured for Shirley to sit on the accent chair to the left of the couch. Shirley succeeded in removing the coat and hung it on the coatrack. She stepped into the living room. Scattered on the coffee table were several brochures. Shirley sat down.

"What is all this, Mother?"

"I'm researching. I need to figure out what to do with you, dear."

"*Do* with me?"

"You're floundering. Ever since you graduated high school more than a year ago, you've done nothing with your life!"

"I want to do something with my life! I want to work for the paper! If anything, you should be sitting Dad down and pestering him to hire me."

Susan's eyes narrowed.

"Listen to me, young lady. Your father has only the best of intentions. He's been the editor of that paper for more than a decade, and he—"

"He's driving it into the ground!" Shirley pounded her fists on the arms of the chair. It was a childish move, she knew, but being around her parents always brought out her juvenile side. "I have more talent in my left hand than Herman Stanley has in his whole body, but who did Dad choose to work for him? You don't see a paycheck coming home with me!"

"Now Shirl, that Stanley boy is a good kid."

"That doesn't make him right for the job! It should have been me. If I'd been born with a different set of parts, you know I'd be working for Dad!"

Susan gasped, but she did not deny the obvious truth of the statement. Instead of replying, she reached for one of the brochures on the table.

"I think there's something we need to discuss," Susan said as she handed the brochure to Shirley. Shirley refused to take it, so Susan opened it, pretending to read the information inside. "There's a very lovely place I think will do you a lot of good. You'll live there for one year and learn all about manners and etiquette, then administrative skills—typing, dictation, shorthand, telephone skills. Then there will be an internship program where they will send you to work in an office in one of the big cities."

"Manners and etiquette? Administrative skills? Mother, I do not want to be a secretary. Nor do I want to stay here and be a goddamn housewife like you!" Shirley's mother winced at this. "I want to be a photographer, and I want to write articles for the paper. I want to do the things I'm good at!"

"Shirley, that role is not a good fit for a young

woman. And if you have your heart set on a man such as Phillip Winfield, there are a lot of, um, *social skills* you need to pick up. Calumet Academy offers it all!"

"Why do you keep bringing up Phillip Winfield?"

"I know all about your obsession, dear. You don't have to be upset. In fact, I had quite an infatuation with his father when I was your age. That Winfield family has wonderful genes. But it's just a young girl's fantasy. You'll never land a high-class man as you are now."

Shirley jumped to her feet. She leaned toward her mother, grabbed the brochure out of the woman's hands, and tore it in half.

"I don't want a sad, sorry existence like yours, Mother. I don't want to settle for some pathetic middle-aged lady's expectations the way you did. I don't want to be you. And I don't want to be a secretary or a teacher or a housewife. I don't want proper manners. I don't want to be forced to marry some sad sack like Herman Stanley and rely on him to take care of my every need for the rest of my life. It makes me sick to think of turning into you!"

Shirley turned and walked out of the living room. The bright yellow coat hanging in the hallway caught her eye. She stopped and stared at it.

Is Herman really so bad? she thought. Surely no boy had ever shown so much interest in her or shared so many of the same hobbies and dreams. He was quite loyal to her. He was gangly and a bit awkward, but he was quite handsome in his own way. She laughed with him at least as much as she laughed at him when they spent time together.

The rapid sniffling sounds her mother made when she cried rose behind her. Shirley moved down the hallway to her room and slammed the door.

Normally, when Shirley had a rough day, she settled on her desk chair or her bed and gazed at the photographs she had snapped of the object of her desire. There was something about Phillip that always calmed her, sent her into pleasant daydreams. Perhaps her mother was right—perhaps it was just a young girl's fantasy, a pathetic infatuation that would never come to fruition. But right now, she didn't care.

However, looking at the pictures wasn't an option on this particular morning.

The pictures were gone.

All of them.

Shirley turned to her shelf where she kept her camera, extra film, flashbulbs, and other accessories. They were all gone.

She opened her door. Her mother was right there, ready for Shirley's response.

"It's for your own good, honey. It's time to move on with your life."

Shirley slammed her shoulder into her mother's as she pushed past the woman and into the hallway. She grabbed the yellow raincoat and ventured back out into the storm on her bicycle. She ignored her mother screaming her name as she rode away from her home.

"Well, well, lover girl," said a snide voice, followed by a snicker Shirley knew all too well.

"Cut it out, Junior." Shirley peeled off the raincoat, hung it on a peg next to the door of the diner, and sat in the nearest booth. She waved away the menu her sneering former classmate attempted to hand her. "Get me a shepherd's pie and a strawberry soda pop. Oh, and a cheeseburger with extra pickles and a side of coleslaw and some ginger ale. Please."

"Coleslaw and extra pickles?" Graham Junior tapped the table with the menu in his hand. "I know exactly who that is for. Trying to impress your daddy's little assistant?"

"Just buzz off before I have to file a complaint with *your* daddy." That was enough to send Graham Junior back behind the counter to put in the order with Raymond, the diner's afternoon short-order cook.

Shirley looked around the place. Unlike the last time she had entered Graham's Diner, Phillip Winfield was nowhere to be found. Not that it was a surprise; the wealthy young man rarely frequented the diner unless he was downtown for another purpose, and even then it was quite rare. He usually had goods brought in from the big city and beyond, as Raventree Hollow wasn't set up to serve those with expensive taste.

Graham Junior walked by and set down a small plate piled high with dill pickle slices. He began to open his mouth when Shirley shot him a look that he wisely took as *Don't you dare speak, boy*. Shirley heard his teeth clatter together as he quickly turned away to tend to another customer instead of antagonizing her further. She pulled one of the pickle slices off the top and pushed the plate to the other side of the table, where Herman would soon be sitting.

As she chewed the pickle slice, wincing from the vinegar, Shirley wondered how old the cucumber it was made from might be. *When was it picked from the vine? Could I be consuming something that's been on this earth as long as I have been? Or even longer?* With proper preservation, handling, and storage, Shirley thought she'd heard that pickled foods could last for decades. Whether anyone would be crazy enough to eat it after all that time was another matter.

This whole town feels like it was soaked in brine and sealed up real tight in a jar, she thought. *Everyone here just goes on living in the same boring ways, day in and day out, with no change. Most of us never leave this place behind. It's like something here has a hold on us, keeps us fed with idle gossip and dysfunctional neighbors, and we never know the difference. We just keep on giving it whatever nutrients it needs to survive, and the cycle continues.*

"Hiya, Shirl," Herman called out. Shirley snapped out of her daze. "Sorry I'm late. I was finishing up the story for the paper."

Shirley looked up at the boy. He was dripping wet. His wool jacket was no match for the storm that was hammering the town.

"Sorry about your coat. I was so preoccupied, I didn't even think to give it back to you."

"That's okay, Shirley, honest. You can keep it until this storm lets up if you want!" Herman sat in front of the plate of pickles. His eyes lit up. "Say, do you mind if I have some of these pickles? I sure love a good pickle."

Shirley laughed at this and snatched one more pickle before leaving him the other dozen slices. She watched his boyish grin as he looked down at the plate. He sure was a dopey boy, she thought, but she was realizing more and more how much comfort he brought her when they were together.

"Lunch is served, Manly Stanley," Graham Junior jested as he set the shepherd's pie and cheeseburger on the table. He returned a few seconds later with the drinks and silverware, gave Herman a punch on the shoulder, and disappeared back behind the counter.

"You know, I'm always quite jealous of people who get the heck out of this town," Shirley said, "but if there's one person I'd be happy to see go, it'd be Junior there."

"Aw, he's not so bad once you get past his personality and that grin on his face that makes you want to slap him," Herman said. Shirley spat out the mouthful of strawberry soda she had just sipped through her straw as she laughed involuntarily.

"I was not expecting that from you of all people," she said. She reached for the napkin Herman handed her and blotted up the sugary drink from the table. "You surprise me sometimes."

Herman turned as red as the beverage in Shirley's glass. A silence stretched between them that was broken by the chime of the bells on the door as a customer entered. Both Herman and Shirley looked at the newcomer and quickly glanced back down at their food.

"Good afternoon, Pastor," the older Graham said as Laurence took a seat in another booth. "What can I get for you today?"

"Tuna fish, mustard, and tomato on rye, please," Laurence said. Shirley didn't think he sounded quite like himself. There was something dark or contemplative in his voice, she was sure of it, though she didn't think others in the establishment could tell. She and Herman were the only ones who knew what dark deeds the holy man was about to undertake.

Shirley leaned closer to Herman.

"Eat up quickly," she whispered. "Once he's done with his lunch, he'll be driving out to the train station. It'll take us longer to get there on our bicycles, so we need a head start."

"Shirl, I've already thought of that. I stopped at home after we parted at the park this morning and borrowed my folks' car. It's down in the lot behind the newspaper office."

Shirley's eyes widened with delight. She stood, leaned across the table, and kissed Herman on the cheek. Then she sat back down and dug her fork into the steaming shepherd's pie.

Graham Herndon Junior whooped loudly from behind the counter.

Chapter Seventeen

Shirley and Herman watched Pastor Laurence open his car door. He was parked along the portion of the curb normally reserved for the town's sole taxicab, which curiously hadn't arrived at what was usually the third-busiest time of day for Leonard, the driver. The pastor hadn't spotted the watchful pair a few dozen feet away in the parking lot, as his eyes were locked on the approaching afternoon train. The brakes squealed loudly as the engine and commuter cars pulled up to the station platform.

The first person off the train was a funny little man whom neither Shirley nor Herman recognized. He was followed by several townspeople the pair didn't think twice about, who pulled up their hoods or unfolded newspapers to shield their heads from the rain. Then came Rebecca Abrams, dressed modestly but quite finely for her surprise reunion with her lover. It seemed she hadn't expected the storm.

"I forgot how gorgeous she is," Shirley said. She hoped Herman could not detect the tinge of jealousy in her voice.

Rebecca stepped down to the platform and waited for the porter to carry her suitcases off of the train. She flashed a genuine smile at the man, but he avoided eye contact with her and quickly stepped back onto the train with no professional courtesy. Shirley knew why. Rebecca would likely receive similar treatment in town should she sit down at Graham's Diner or ask for a trim at Frank's Barber Shop. Raventree Hollow was almost entirely white. The progressive influence of the big city hadn't yet seeped into the fabric of society, especially among the older population of the town. There hadn't been a single person of color in Shirley's class in all her years of school. It was another strike against Raventree Hollow in Shirley's growing collection of frustrations.

"Let me give you a hand with that, Ms. Abrams," a voice called out. It was Pastor Laurence hollering from the curb. He jogged up the steps and across the platform to Rebecca. He popped open his umbrella and handed it to the young woman.

Shirley couldn't hear what they were saying all the way from the parking lot. She witnessed a handshake, friendly smiles on both faces, and Rebecca laughing at something the pastor said. Rebecca looked around, probably to confirm that no taxi was present, and then glanced down at her luggage, which she allowed Laurence to carry for her. She followed him down to his car, where Laurence opened the door for her and then loaded the luggage into the trunk.

"Well, maybe you're right, Shirley," Herman said softly. The disappointment in his voice broke Shirley's heart. "Perhaps the good pastor isn't so good after all."

Laurence closed the trunk and walked toward the driver's side door of his car. He opened it but looked around the station before getting in. His gaze stopped on Shirley and Herman. Unsure of what else to do, Shirley reached over and pulled Herman in for a surprise kiss. Her eyes were still open, and she looked at Herman, whose eyes were wide with shock. In her peripheral vision, she saw Pastor Laurence shutting his door and starting the engine. Once he pulled away from the curb, Shirley unlocked her lips from Herman's and gently pushed him away. She settled back into the passenger seat.

"Wow. What... what..." was all Herman could muster.

"Go, Herman! Follow him!"

"But... but I... we..."

"It was nothing! I had to do something when he

spotted us. Sorry if I was forceful, Herman." Shirley laughed as he continued to gape at her. "I mean, you are a wonderful kisser, but I meant nothing by it. Now, please, let's not lose the pastor's car!"

Herman turned back toward the steering wheel, started the ignition, and rubbed his burning red cheeks. He backed out of the spot without looking, but fortunately, the lot was fairly empty. Once on the main road, he sped up until Pastor Laurence's sedan was in view.

"Well, gee, Shirley," he said, a smile breaking out on his face, "you're sure a quick thinker!"

"Slow down just a bit, Herman. We don't want to get too close, or he may realize we're following him."

They continued down the road with just enough distance between the cars to make Shirley comfortable. The pastor's car made a left turn at an intersection in town.

"Where's he going now?" Herman asked.

"I think he's avoiding Main Street," Shirley said. "He'll cut through the residential streets so there's less chance of being seen by the townspeople. Let's turn right instead, then go up Palmdale. We know his destination, so we may as well not let him catch us weaving through all the neighborhoods behind him."

Herman followed her instructions. The accident from earlier that morning had cleared up, and it was smooth sailing without the afternoon pedestrian traffic they would have encountered on Main Street.

Once they had bypassed the primary shopping district, Herman made a left turn and cut across Main, heading west toward the hill on which the convent loomed over the town.

"I've never been up there before," Herman said. The fear in his voice was obvious to Shirley.

"I don't think anybody really has. Just look at this road!"

Eldridge Valley Road wasn't exclusive to the convent. It followed the curves of the hill and wound through sections of trees, alongside a creek, and up to a few farms on the outskirts of town. That said, it wasn't maintained as well as other roads in town, as the low volume of traffic didn't justify pouring funds into keeping it up. Herman leaned forward, his head over the steering wheel, foot rapidly alternating between gas pedal and brake. Between the wet road and the blind turns, it was a sketchy several minutes at best.

"If only there was a direct route up the hill," Shirley said, "but you're doing a fine job regardless."

The road snaked all the way around the hill before they reached the steep turnoff that led up to the convent's long driveway. She saw Herman relax as they approached.

"Well, here we are!"

"Wait! Don't turn just yet, Herman. We need to pass it and pull off ahead. There's no way the pastor beat us here, and if we turn up that road first, we won't be able to hide."

"But don't we want to stop him from bringing Rebecca into the convent?" Herman drove past the turnoff and found a shoulder wide enough to pull off the road around the next bend.

"If the nuns are in on this, they'll far outnumber us," Shirley said. "We need to go in covertly."

Shirley hopped out of the car and backtracked up the road on foot.

"Wait up!" Herman jumped out and followed her. As they approached the bend, they left the road and hiked up the hill several yards under the cover of the trees. They were walking parallel to the muddy unpaved driveway when the sound of Pastor Laurence's car met their ears. Shirley and Herman dropped into the brush. Once the car passed, they continued up the hill.

"He's doing it," Herman whispered. "He's really doing it."

As they followed the driveway up and around a bend, they caught Laurence's voice.

"Please, just trust me on this," he was saying to a handful of elderly nuns who had opened one of the looming gates. A high stone wall circled the entire property as if this was a fortress to be protected. "Just one or two nights maximum, and I will be back to see this through."

The pair couldn't make out what the nuns were saying, nor could they see the women's expressions in the shadows of their veils. Rebecca's silhouette was visible in the passenger seat, and Shirley thought the young woman was crying from the tremble of her shoulders and head.

"The car is still running," Herman whispered. "Maybe we can run up, jump in, and drive her back down to safety."

"Herman, that won't work. They'll catch us on the approach. There isn't enough cover between the tree line and the car. They'll grab us and lock us up in a cell with Rebecca. We'll have to come back when they are least expecting it."

They watched as Pastor Laurence returned to his car. The gates opened wider, and Pastor Laurence pulled inside before they slammed shut again.

"Come on," Shirley said, not waiting for Herman as she descended the hill. Herman followed her back to the car without a word. As they neared Eldridge Valley Road again, Pastor Laurence's car rolled through the intersection and turned back toward town, and they dropped down instinctively. Once he was out of sight, they rushed to Herman's father's car, soaked from head to toe from the downpour.

"Well, what now?"

"We need a better understanding of that place if we're going to sneak in," Shirley said. "What to expect. Where they may lock her up."

"Do you know anyone who's been there that we could ask?"

"I don't know that anyone in town has ever been allowed into the convent. Pastor Laurence may have just gotten closest."

"We should just go to Sheriff Holman," Herman conceded.

"I have a better idea," Shirley said. "Take us to the library."

Chapter Eighteen

Shirley jumped out of the car while it was still in motion as Herman struggled to parallel park.

"*God love it*, Shirley! You can't do that while I'm still driving," Herman called.

"You turned a parking job into a twelve-point turn, Herman! You were moving at a snail's pace. Now, shut off the engine and let's go."

Shirley slammed the door and jogged up the steps to the town's library. It was a large two-story affair at the north end of Main Street, just before the road ended at the apple orchards owned by Jimmy Weiland. Throughout her childhood and teen years, the place had been like a second home to Shirley. If she didn't have her eye up to the viewfinder of a camera, she certainly had her nose in a book. There was a particular thrill she got every time she walked through the heavy double doors and into the house of knowledge and wonder. She knew she'd soon be whisked away to another land, a place far from Raventree Hollow, and see the world through the eyes of a person who wasn't bound by the shackles of Shirley's own life. There was something that felt so secret about it. Scandalous, even.

The librarians, Mr. Olsen and Ms. Dotson, were full of scandals themselves. They weren't married to each other, and they kept separate homes, but everyone in town knew they spent most nights together. Both had been widowed in middle age, and their long hours together in the library and their shared loneliness had naturally drawn them together. But the scandals didn't end there. They were also fond of what the townspeople considered lowbrow literature. Filth. Satanic stories. Fantasy and horror. Time travel. Tales of other worlds, of monsters and demons and barbarians. And Shirley basked in it all when she visited the library, where nobody judged her.

It was the perfect place for outcasts and misfits, for girls like Shirley and boys like young Arnie McCann. It was fitting, then, that those two misfits greeted each other in the institution's foyer.

"Welcome to Raventree Public Library," Arnie recited.

"Your gateway to a thousand worlds," Shirley finished. She knew the line well. It was a favorite of Mr. Olsen, who loved greeting patrons at the door before guiding them to their books of interest. "Good afternoon, Arnie. Is Mr. Olsen here?"

"He and Ms. Dotson are out of town this week for, uh, a publishing trade show. I can, um, I can help you, though." The boy pushed up his cola-bottle spectacles and smiled proudly.

"Wow, they put you in charge? Well, good for you, Arnie! Twelve years old, and already head librarian!"

"Fourteen, actually. And I'm just a, um, a volunteer."

The door opened again, and Herman entered along with a gust of warm, soggy air.

"Gee, that storm just won't let up," Herman said. "Hiya, Arnie!"

Shirley took one glance at Herman and rolled her eyes. "Glad you finally managed to park the car on that empty street, Herman." She turned back to Arnie. "Could you take me to the books on local history?"

"Local history? Uh, like, about Raventree Hollow? Well..." Arnie looked toward the shelves. "I don't think you'll find anything here. There isn't much about this town that would fill a book."

"You can say that again," Herman said.

"Not now, Herman. This is important." Shirley

shook her head. "How far back do the newspaper archives go, Arnie?"

The boy led Shirley toward the back right corner of the building. Instead of wooden bookshelves loaded with bound volumes, this area was filled with heavy filing cabinets. Arnie stopped at the first one and opened the top drawer.

"These are the oldest. The *Raventree Herald* was founded in 1903 after the *Kings Valley Chronicle* went out of business. The *Chronicle* issues we have date back to, um, let's see..." Arnie reached to the back of the drawer and pulled out a plastic sleeve with a tattered yellow piece of newspaper in it. The print had almost completely faded, but a much more recent label was affixed to the plastic that held it. "Eighteen forty-eight, it says."

Shirley reached across the open drawer and took the plastic-encased newspaper clipping from Arnie. The top headline was still legible. She read it aloud. "Gold Discovered in California! Local Treasure Hunters Pack Wagons and Head West." Shirley slipped the newspaper back into its place and carefully shuffled through the other clipping around it. "It's only national news. Nothing local!"

"I think whoever saved these didn't care about local news," Arnie observed. "You know how this town is. People always know everything. There wasn't any use documenting the gossip, or at least not saving it here."

Shirley slammed the drawer and leaned against the cabinet with her arms crossed. Arnie and Herman looked at her in silence for a moment before the younger boy spoke up.

"What is it that you want to learn about?" Arnie asked. "I kind of... well, I know quite a lot about local history from my grandmother."

"Your grandmother? Listen, Arnie, I can't listen to old wives' tales right now. There are some important things I need to find out about."

"Well, uh, my grandmother was a bit of a historian. Granddad wouldn't let her publish any of her writing because he didn't think it was, um, a woman's place. So instead, she always told me what she learned in her research. I remember most of it. I, uh, I'm kind of a genius, you know."

"Wow, that sounds swell, Arnie," Herman said. "I'd sure like to hear what you know. What do you say, Shirley? Can we sit and listen to what he has to tell us?"

Shirley sighed and relented. She walked over to one of the study tables. Herman and Arnie joined her.

"What in particular do you want to know about?" Arnie asked.

"The Convent of the Sisters of Mercy up the hill. Did your grandmother say anything about that?"

Arnie gasped.

"I, um, yes. But I don't know if there's any truth to it. I should probably mention that Grandmother Gertrude was very intelligent, but she also sometimes seemed to mix things up. Sometimes I was sure she was adding elements from books she read. Fiction. Especially when she talked about the convent."

"That's okay." Herman patted the kid on the back. "We'll listen to whatever you know and appreciate it all the same."

"Well, um, okay. She told me that place wasn't built for the nuns, that the Catholic Church had nothing to do with its construction. I, um, can't remember where she said the family who built it was from. Eastern Europe is the best I can do. They were big-time royalty in their country."

"Like a king or an emperor?" Herman asked.

"Of course not, Herman," Shirley said. "We would know if a king had crossed the Atlantic and made his home in Raventree Hollow, of all places. Go on, Arnie."

"I... I think more like a duke or a governor, but he certainly had the wealth of a king. I don't know if Grandmother knew why the family left Europe if they had so much money and power."

"A civil war, perhaps, or a coup that put them in

danger," Herman said, and Shirley couldn't help but giggle at the pride on the young man's face. He caught her eye and blushed.

"I think you're right, Herman," Arnie said. "Something made them flee with whatever money they could get their hands on and hide."

"What makes you think they hid, Arnie?" Shirley asked.

"Um, well, like you said earlier, they came to Raventree Hollow, of all places. They could have gone to a big coastal city. Boston, perhaps. Instead, they traveled inland to these parts. When they arrived, there was no town here. The Tahinee tribe controlled most of the valley. A couple of white settler families had claimed patches of land nearby, but the hills were empty. The family had a choice: eastern hill or western hill."

"They chose wrong," Shirley said.

"Indeed. The Tahinee folks tried to warn them to avoid the western hill. Said there were evil spirits living in its depths. The head of the family—Josef, I think his name was—laughed it off. He claimed it was evidence the western hill was a prime location, that perhaps there were even precious metals deep within it or something else the natives didn't want to give up. The family set up camp on the hill while Josef headed back east to hire builders and source materials.

"Peter, the second-oldest son, went with his father, while the oldest son, Tristan, and his wife and three young children stayed behind with his mother and twin teenage sisters. They had brought shovels and other tools with them to flatten the hilltop and get it ready for their home's foundation. That's when things started to go wrong. Very, very wrong."

"Don't tell me the Indians attacked," Herman said.

"Not at all. As I said before, the Tahinee avoided the land. They left the family alone and moved their own camps farther away from the base of the hill. They wanted no part in it. As the more capable family members worked on the foundation, the younger children explored the area. On the southeast section of the hilltop, they stumbled upon a patch of large rocks that didn't appear to be native to the hill. There were no others like them anywhere else in the region. It was as if someone had brought them in and stacked them to cover up something in the ground.

"The children were bright enough to realize the rocks were hiding something but not wise enough to leave them alone. They were curious, as children are. They pulled up one rock, and another, and another, and stacked them to one side. Soon they discovered that under the rocks was a layer of tree trunks that had been bundled together to make a platform about as big as the floor of a banquet hall."

"None of the adults noticed the children were doing this?" Shirley asked.

"They were too consumed with digging out the foundation before Josef returned with the builders. This was over a period of several days or weeks, mind you. The children were working just as hard as the adults."

"I wonder if the Tahinee built the platform and brought in the rocks to hide it," Herman said. "Maybe it was some religious site or burial ground."

"No," Arnie said bluntly. "As I said, the Tahinee avoided the hilltop at all costs. I believe they'd avoided it for generations and didn't even know why, just that it was something that had always been done. From what Grandmother said, the wood was quite ancient even back then.

"The children continued to explore. They snuck off with some of the shovels and other tools. They pried and hacked at the wooden platform. As they chipped away at it, an odor wafted up through the new cracks, rot and decay that had not been exposed to fresh air for millennia. Yet it didn't deter the children. Piece by piece, they opened a hole in the wood. Then there was a groan as the wood flexed, bowed, and caved in."

"Those poor children!" Herman exclaimed.

"Only one of them," Arnie said. "The other two jumped away just in time, but one little boy was right in the center of the platform. Several moments after it collapsed and plunged into darkness, taking the boy with it, the other children heard a splash deep inside the hill. They yelled down for their brother, but there was no answer, just a gurgling as the wood sank into the liquid below.

"They ran and retrieved their parents. Tristan, their father, was quick to act. He grabbed a rope and tied one end to a sturdy tree nearby and the other end around himself. The rest of the family lowered him down, but the rope wasn't long enough. The hole seemed as it if it went all the way to the bottom of the hill. He called up to let them know he thought there were enough nooks and crannies in the walls to climb down without the rope. A few moments later, they heard Tristan scream, followed by a splash, more gurgling sounds, and then nothing."

"He and the child were just gone?" Shirley asked.

"A few days later, Josef returned with a large team of builders and a wagon train of supplies. Before they started building their new estate, they chopped down the tallest trees they could find in the valley and built a new platform to cover the pit. The home they built was a replica of the castle they had fled in their old country: outer walls, bell tower, and all."

"You said the pit was in the southeast corner?" Shirley asked. "That's where the bell tower is."

"Yes. Perhaps they shouldn't have been so

faithful to the original design, though—it was at their own peril that they included that part of the castle. They should have listened to the natives and left that land alone. As the years trudged on, tragedy struck nearly every member of the family. Even the laborers were not spared; dozens died in construction accidents. Josef's wife, Maria, had horrible nightmares every single night. Just months after they completed the castle, Maria murdered Josef in their bed and then hung herself in the bell tower. As was customary in their culture, the second-oldest son, Peter, married his older brother's widow and became responsible for the surviving children. He wasn't much of a leader, though. He spent his days and nights in the bell tower, pacing back and forth as if something connected him to whatever was below it.

"One night, when his new bride came to him and begged him to join her in their marriage bed, he attacked her with his bare hands. His twin sisters ran down the hill and begged one of the neighboring settlers and a few of the Tahinee men to help them. The group of men hiked up to the castle and found Peter with a knife, carving into the fresh corpse of his wife and consuming pieces of the body. They put him down with a gun one man had brought."

"Arnie, this is so horrible," Herman said. Shirley thought he was crying, but he had turned away from her to hide the tears. "How could any of this be true? Why would your grandmother tell you such a tale?"

"Because it *is* true. I think so, anyway. Grandmother wanted to warn me. That place is evil, and she didn't want me to ever go near it."

"How can it be evil, though?" Shirley asked. "Why would nuns live there now if it was some satanic place?"

"To protect us from whatever evil is contained there. Peter's sisters, the two surviving children, and the servants who lived with them in the castle abandoned the place after that. They moved over to the eastern hill—"

"Where the Winfield estate is?" Shirley asked.

"Exactly. The Tahinee and the nearby settlers all pitched in to build a small home for the survivors. There was plenty of money for the supplies. The sisters spent time in the city, and one of them eventually married a man, a Winfield. That was the start of the Winfield line we know.

"But on the western hill, evil still lurked. The Winfields brought in the Catholic Church. For many years, several priests lived there. I don't know when they put the nuns into place, but they've been there ever since. Trying to contain whatever evil lives below, I suppose. According to Grandmother, the nuns might be under some kind of mind control. She thought the reason they don't come down to the town is that they've become attached to whatever evil entity is up there, and they can't leave it. They feed it, or it feeds them. Day in, day out."

"And then what?" Herman asked.

"That's it. That's the story Grandmother told me. That's all I know."

Shirley and Herman stared at each other in disbelief. The silence continued for several minutes as they both replayed the story in their minds like some deranged snuff film.

Finally, Shirley stood up.

"What are you doing, Shirl?" Herman asked.

"Going back up there. We can't let them kill Rebecca Abrams."

Shirley grabbed Herman's keys from his hand, walked across the library, and disappeared into the rain without a look back at the boys.

Chapter Nineteen

That rotten, insufferable little lady, Shirley Bettencourt, was right there.

Right where Agnes Butterfield knew she'd be.

Right where...

Where what?

Where the voices said she'd be.

Yes, there were *voices* telling Agnes to wait outside the library and catch the meddler. Voices that both soothed and ignited the fire within Agnes's head. Coaxing. Controlling. Lovingly demanding. Sensually titillating her curiosity. Horrible but beautiful. She despised them for the things they'd made her do so far, and yet she loved and valued them to the depths of her soul.

She had to keep feeding them. She had to do what they said. And just now, they'd said to do this.

"Hello, deary," Agnes said—syrupy sweet or bitterly phony, she didn't quite know, but it didn't matter. The two words had their effect. The girl stopped on the sidewalk as if an invisible hand had grabbed her. Shirley dropped the keys she was holding, right hand frozen in a claw position. The girl's head shook and shivered as if she was fighting for control of her neck, and then her eyes met Agnes's.

"What... what are you doing here?" Shirley asked, her voice quivering as much as the rest of her.

"I need you to join me back at my inn, my girl. Your work there was unfinished when you stormed off last week. You owe it to a little disabled woman such as me."

"I... No. No! What are you doing to me?" Shirley's feet started to move in Agnes's direction. Her eyes remained locked on the woman in the wheelchair, whom she followed through the rain. The inn was only one block away, and Agnes hoped there would be no witnesses to their odd little procession.

"Come along." Agnes reached into her coat and pulled out a flask of bourbon. She stopped wheeling long enough to down its contents, which was just enough time for the girl to involuntarily catch up. "Give me a push, girl."

Shirley complied. She guided the wheelchair up

the ramp of the Raventree Inn and through the front door.

"Go ahead and lock it, Ms. Bettencourt. Don't miss any of the bolts. We don't want any disturbances."

Again, Shirley complied involuntarily.

Agnes giggled softly as she heard the first lock click behind her. She cackled at the second lock. By the time Shirley got to the top deadbolt, the woman was roaring with vivacious, sinister laughter. Tears poured down her cheeks. A cramp in her belly caused her to bend forward, and she fell out of the wheelchair. She gasped for air, but it was no use—the laughter kept coming. She rolled onto her back and pounded her fists on the floor. Through her tears, she could make out the confused, submissive girl standing over her, unable to move of her own free will. It only made Agnes laugh harder.

Once she had regained control of herself, she sat up and climbed into the wheelchair again. She repositioned it to face Shirley.

"You will climb the stairs to the third floor. Go to room three oh four. The door is open, but it will lock behind you when you close it. You will remain there until the deeds are done and it is convenient for you to leave again. Do you understand me, you stupid little bitch?"

"I... yes." The girl looked like a mindless creature,

a scarecrow missing its brain. As she passed Agnes, the woman spat up at her from the wheelchair. The spittle hit Shirley's left cheek, and Shirley stopped in her tracks. Her head vibrated again as if it was trying to turn, but she couldn't fight off whatever was controlling her. Without a word, Shirley began walking again. She headed up the two flights of stairs and slammed the door.

Agnes began to laugh again. She couldn't stop it. She fell to the floor once more and wriggled around. Drool seeped from the corners of her lips and down her cheeks. The cramp in her stomach quickly returned, and it soon evolved into a pain. She pissed herself. And still the laughter continued.

"Agnes, my dear, what are you doing on the floor?"

Agnes wiped the tears from her eyes. For a moment, she thought, *Yes, just what the hell* am *I doing on the floor?* And then, as if a cloud had rolled through the sky and blanketed the sun, a veil seemed to cover her conscience once again.

"Ronnie Marie. The old maid. What the hell are you doing here, wench?" Agnes reached up for Ronnie Marie's assistance.

"Aggie? What's going on with you? Has something happened here? The front door was all bolted, so I had to come in through the kitchen." Ronnie Marie helped pull the woman up and into her chair, but it wasn't an easy feat. It almost felt like moving a recently deceased corpse; the escape of a soul caused a body to double in weight, as if something were pulling it down into the depths of the earth. "Your clothes are soiled, dear. Let's get you to your room to change your—"

Ronnie Marie broke off when she heard a loud thud from somewhere upstairs.

"Ignore it," Agnes said as she wheeled down the hall toward the kitchen.

"Were you attacked? It sounds like someone's still in the house! Let's get out of here, Agnes. I don't like this one bit."

Ronnie Marie realized she was now alone in the hallway. She darted into the kitchen after her friend.

"It's nothing," Agnes said. She ignited the gas range and set the kettle on for tea. "I wasn't attacked. There's a pesky little rat of a girl up there who is getting what she deserves. She's been meddling in things that aren't her business."

"You've locked someone up?" Ronnie Marie set out two saucers and a pair of teacups and measured out the scoops of tea by habit despite her apprehen-sion. She dropped the measuring spoon at the sound of a scream from upstairs. "Lord Almighty! Is that the Bettencourt girl?"

Agnes moved away from her, but Ronnie Marie still saw the woman's wicked smile. Agnes rolled to the icebox and pulled out two cakes wrapped in cellophane. She turned and tossed them onto the large butcher block in the center of the kitchen.

"Damn it all, Agnes. This has gone too far! I'm afraid of what these rumors—and the little games you've created around them—are doing to you and to the rest of this town!"

"And who is going to stop me, Ronnie Marie? You? My best friend, the spineless little coward? Run off to Mommy, why don't you. Look at you. The sun is waning on your insignificant life, and you've never been with a man. Never had a propitious moment. Never stood up to anyone, especially not that dying sack of pus that is your mother. You just go off to the city every week to sit at her decaying side. What good has it done you, living for others?"

"That's my mother you're talking about, Agnes! I don't like this path you are on at all!"

"Ha! Listen to me, and listen well. I've lived my life for others before. I loved a man, married him, did things his way. What did it get me?" Agnes gestured around at the dusty, oversize kitchen of the inn. "Abandoned. Stuck with this run-down excuse for a hotel in this backwater town with five hundred boring, predictable, useless humans. Five hundred and one, that is, when you're in town."

"But... but..." Ronnie Marie sobbed. She swept her arm across the butcher block, sending the teacups and saucers across the kitchen. They shattered on the floor. "How dare you speak to me this way, Agnes? I've always loved you like a sister! I've stood by you in good times and bad! I was at the altar on your wedding day. I was here during your miscarriage and when your husband left you for—"

"Don't you dare say that woman's name, Ronnie Marie. And the only thing you've ever done for me was nag, nag, nag. You've always used me to feel like you had some kind of life outside of your mother. But do you know what? You bore me. Your life is so pathetic, it rubs off on anyone you come into contact with. I want no more of it."

"Agnes, you don't know what you're saying! Let me call Doctor Chou and see if he has some kind of medication for—"

"You'd love that, wouldn't you? To have the good doctor drug me up, maybe even commit me to a padded room? Then you could walk around town telling everyone how well you cared for me, just like you did for your mother. Well, my old friend, that's not going to happen." Agnes reached toward the knife block on the counter. She was just able to reach the end of the handle of a steak knife.

"What are you doing?" Ronnie Marie asked. She backed away from the butcher block and inched toward the door behind her.

Agnes pulled the knife from the block. She looked at her old friend with eyes that seemed unfamiliar to Ronnie Marie. Full of hatred. Full of primordial evil. Agnes bent her arm, then flung the knife toward Ronnie Marie.

Ronnie Marie started to turn, but she slipped on the broken saucers on the ground. The knife was inching closer to her by the millisecond, her body tumbling backward. She hit the swinging door, which gave way and opened into the dining room. When she looked up, the steak knife was embedded in the door at the same level her face had been at only moments before.

Ronnie Marie got to her feet quickly and ran out to the foyer. She unbolted all the locks and yanked open the front door. She heard the screams of the girl upstairs, but that would have to be someone else's problem. Ronnie Marie's instinct told her that she had to flee the town and all the evil that had overtaken it.

And so she ran.

Chapter Twenty

The afternoon seemed to drag on in Katrina's shop. Eleanor Trestle and Isabelle Jackson had come in together at one point, seemingly more to gossip than to actually purchase anything. But when they'd been met with Katrina's vacant stares and one-word responses, their smiles had quickly faded, and they had picked out one scented candle each, paid, and promptly left. The storm had kept everyone else away, and Katrina was just fine with that.

What she had said to the girl, how dismissive she had been, it wasn't like her. Shirley wouldn't have lied about what she had overheard between Larry and Agnes, and Katrina knew it. It was just that she didn't want to admit it. Something truly evil had come over Larry, and it was eating away at Katrina.

There was more to it, though. The way his actions hurt her so deeply and continued to taint her thoughts could only mean one thing: She was in love with Larry. Sure, she had *loved* him for years as her oldest and dearest friend, but this wasn't that. This was a deep longing for the man, a feeling that she wasn't complete without him, that his destructive behavior could only mean her destruction as well.

And because she loved Larry, if Agnes Butterfield was indeed corrupting him, she had an obligation to do something about it. She needed to help pull Larry out of his mess, for herself as much as for him.

Katrina flipped the sign in her window, pulled the door closed behind her, and locked it. She may miss out on a customer or two, but it didn't matter to her. Agnes Butterfield was out there, and Katrina had to confront her.

Despite the rain, she peeled out of her driveway in the old coupe she had inherited from her deceased parents. Raindrops covered the windshield, which did not have working wipers. Even if it had, the tears in her eyes still would've obscured her vision.

Is it too late? Katrina wondered. *Has Larry already been irreversibly corrupted by Agnes?*

She turned into the alley in order to avoid the afternoon traffic on Main Street and skidded over the loose gravel as she braked behind the Raventree Inn. Mud splattered from under her tires and painted the fence a filthy brown. She reached for her umbrella on the passenger seat and stepped into the rain, getting soaked in the moment it took her to open it. With the heat she felt from her anger and worry, she didn't mind.

A narrow concrete path led from the alley gate through the weed-choked garden of the inn's neglected backyard and up to the side door. There was a light on in the kitchen, shining through the dreariness of the storm. As Katrina started down the path, a scream caused her to halt. The only other light on in the building was on the third floor, but Katrina couldn't see anyone in the window.

She collapsed her umbrella as she huddled under the overhang on the back porch and turned the door-knob. It opened with a soft click. Katrina started at what she saw.

In the middle of the kitchen, Agnes was asleep in her wheelchair, head tilted toward her right shoulder, drool stretched from lips to elbow. A bottle of bourbon was wedged between the woman's thighs as if they were a makeshift cupholder. On the butcher block in front of her, an open flask lay on its side. Pieces of broken teacups and matching saucers were scattered across the floor. Farther back, a knife protruded from the swinging door to the dining room.

A thud sounded somewhere upstairs, followed by a faint cry. Katrina tiptoed around the table and made her way to the swinging doors. She slowly pushed one open, hoping the creaking of the hinges would not wake the proprietor sleeping a few feet away. As she stepped into the dining room and guided the door closed, she hesitated for a moment, her eyes locked on the knife. Her hand floated toward it. Her fingers were inches away.

"Don't even think about it, deary."

Katrina turned. Agnes was awake and wheeling across the kitchen toward her. Something about the woman's movements seemed off to Katrina. Slow. Crooked. The wheelchair wasn't moving in a straight line because Agnes's arms weren't working in concert with each other.

"Stay away, Ms. Butterfield," Katrina said. Agnes cackled. There was another scream from upstairs, accompanied by a loud thud. "Who is that? Who do you have locked up in this place?"

"Why don't you go upstairs and join her?" Agnes held out a ring of keys. As repulsed as Katrina was by the woman, something made her reach for the keys. She tried to will herself to stop, but she couldn't. She took one step toward Agnes, then a second.

No, this isn't right, she thought. *Stop it!*

"Come, come, Ms. Givens. Come and get it."

Katrina was just a step away when she realized that Agnes's other hand was wrapped around the neck of the bourbon bottle. As Agnes's arm arced back to swing the bottle at her, Katrina regained control of her body. She lashed out with a kick faster than the drunk old woman could move. Her foot firmly struck Agnes's chest, and the woman tipped backward in her wheelchair. The back of Agnes's head hit the tile floor, and her eyes rolled back.

Katrina lunged forward, grabbed the keys, and ran to the dining room, pulling the knife out of the door with her free hand. She darted across the dining room, down the hall, and up two flights of stairs.

The first three doors she passed on the third floor were open. In the stormy dimness of the early evening, she could just make out the interiors of the abandoned rooms. *How long has it been since any of these were occupied?* she wondered. *It's been months since anyone stayed here.* The smell of must and dust was strong. Agnes had been in the wheelchair for a few weeks and thus hadn't been able to clean the rooms upstairs, but it seemed like it had been much longer since anyone had entered them.

Except one room.

At the end of the hall, light streamed from under the only closed door, which was adorned with a small placard labeled 304.

"Hello? Is someone out there?" The girlish voice was unmistakable.

"Shirley? It's Katrina. I'm going to get you out of there!"

She glanced down and fumbled with the keys. Each had a room number engraved on it, and she found the right one. It was a tough fit—it seemed it hadn't been used in so long that the lock had warped—but she forced it in and turned it from side to side until she finally felt a click. The door flew open as the girl pulled from the other side. Katrina and Shirley embraced.

"Oh, Katrina, thank you so much! I thought I was going to die and rot in this dreadful place!"

"How did you even get in there? Agnes can't climb the stairs. Is someone helping her?"

"I don't know how to explain it. I didn't have control over my body or mind. Somehow, I complied with whatever she told me to do. It was absolutely horrible!"

Katina left the keys hanging from the rusted lock and grabbed Shirley's hand with her left, still gripping the knife in her right. "Come on, then. Let's get out of here while we still can."

"Where's Agnes?" Shirley asked. She hesitated despite Katrina's attempt to pull her down the hall. "She's going to do it again. She's going to stop me and send me back up here."

"Shirley, I knocked her down. She hit her head. I think we're safe. We won't know for sure until we get down the stairs, but I have this!" She lifted the knife to show the frightened young woman.

"Okay, I guess." Shirley started walking, slowly at first, but she picked up her pace after a few steps.

At the top of the stairs, they both halted at a creaking sound below. Shirley leaned close to Kat and whispered, "She's down there. She's coming for us."

Katrina patted the girl's shoulder. "No, Shirley, she's injured. She can't climb the stairs, remember? We'll be okay."

She led Shirley down the first set of stairs. They paused on the landing of the second floor and listened, but they were met only by silence.

One step down, then another. And then something creaked again... from behind them.

Katrina turned just as Agnes flew out of the shadows, lunging through the air from the second-floor landing. Kat threw herself between Shirley and the madwoman. Agnes swung her bourbon bottle, which connected with the side of Kat's head and shattered just before the woman's full weight slammed into her. The knife flew over the railing and plummeted into the darkness below.

Shirley screamed but was able to dart out of the way before the two older women came crashing down on her. Katrina did her best to keep her balance, but it was useless. She fell backward onto the railing, then tumbled over it with Agnes. As they fell, she grabbed her attacker's coat and twisted on top of her. Agnes struck the hardwood floor first and cushioned her landing, and once again, Katrina saw the woman's eyes roll back into her head.

"Oh my God! Kat!" Katrina turned to see Shirley rushing down the last few steps and hurtling over the upended wheelchair at the bottom. She helped Katrina to her feet. "Are you okay?"

Katrina looked down at Agnes, who was passed out. "Better than her," she said. The knife had landed inches away from Agnes, so Katrina kicked it away. "I guess she climbed the stairs after all, despite her condition. It's as if her pure hatred gave her the strength."

Katrina grabbed Shirley's hand again, and they took two steps toward the door before she stumbled.

"You need to slow down, Kat," Shirley said. "You're bleeding."

Katrina reached up to the side of her head where the bourbon bottle had connected. Sure enough, a shard of glass had torn a gash from her temple to just millimeters from her eye. She plucked a small piece of the bottle from her skin and dropped it to the floor. "I'll be okay."

They cut through the kitchen and out the back door to Katrina's car in the alleyway.

"Let's get you to the sheriff," Katrina said as she started the car.

"No," Shirley said. "There's someone else in much more danger than I was. We have to rescue her right away, and I don't think we can wait for anybody else in this town to help us."

Chapter Twenty-One

Katrina pushed the gas pedal to the floor. The alley wasn't crowded, so she didn't fear sideswiping any parked cars or running down any pedestrians. She wasn't normally a wild driver, especially not during a storm, but if what Shirley had said was true, there was a girl in danger, and Kat's friend—*lover?*—had been responsible for it. So, caution and speed limits be damned, Katrina pressed forward.

And then the bicycle appeared.

She hadn't even noticed it approaching. The rain was coming down fast, obscuring her view through the windshield, and the steam rising from Kat and her companion was fogging up the windows from the inside. It was Shirley's scream that drew her attention to the bike, but by the time her brain processed it, the car had already crushed it. Kat hit the brakes, and they skidded twenty feet to a halt.

"Oh my God," Shirley cried, gripping the door handle. "Did we just—"

"I didn't even see it coming," Katrina said. "It didn't look like anyone was riding it."

Katrina opened her door and jumped out into the rain. There was no one else in the alley. She ran behind the car. There on the rough gravel, hanging from the car's undercarriage, was what remained of a child's bicycle.

"There's no blood," Shirley said. She was down on her knees in the gravel, looking under the car. "No body, either."

Katrina ran back to where she thought the collision had occurred. No children were lying on the ground. There was no little boy or girl hiding among the trash cans or peeking over any of the low fences that lined the narrow road.

"Did someone push the bike and run away?" Katrina asked. "Why would anyone do such a thing?"

"It's trying to stop us. It knows we're coming."

Katrina turned toward Shirley in confusion. "Who? Who is trying to stop us?"

"Something evil. The same thing that has a hold on Agnes Butterfield. The same thing that has a hold on your Laurence."

Her Laurence. Katrina liked the sound of that,

even if it was scandalous. But no, now was not the time.

"Well, let's disappoint this thing, then," Kat said.

She ran back to the rear bumper of her car, where she and Shirley wrestled the frame of the bicycle until it came free. She tossed it off to the side of the road, into a heap of weeds and milk crates, and got back in the car.

They sped down the rest of the alley and turned onto the main road, heading toward the western outskirts of town. At every intersection, they came across pedestrians making their way leisurely across the street.

"I've never seen so many people out walking in the middle of a storm before," Katrina said as she floored it across an intersection after old Ms. Merriweather had finished her sloth-paced journey across Camellia Drive. "Is this also part of the evil thing's plan to stop us?"

Shirley laughed nervously but didn't reply. Katrina looked over to make sure the girl was okay. That's when she saw fear strike the girl's face like a bolt of lightning.

"Watch out!" Shirley screamed.

Kat hit the brakes instinctively just as one of the tall magnolia trees that lined the road crashed to the pavement directly in front of them. The tires squealed across the water-slick street as the car came to a stop a mere inch from the corpse of the tree.

Kat put the car in reverse, backed up twenty feet, and gave the wheel a hard yank to the left. She sped over the lawn of the Ellerbee house, crushing Francine Ellerbee's prize daffodils, which lined the sidewalk. Once they were on the other side of the fallen tree, she resumed her cruising speed toward the outskirts of Raventree Hollow.

Shirley laughed again, but this time Kat didn't think it sounded as nervous as before. It was the adrenaline. Katrina felt the rush as well. She laughed along with the girl.

IN HER ENTIRE LIFETIME IN RAVENTREE HOLLOW, Katrina Givens had never once sat in traffic on the winding road that led west from the town. She thought she recognized Hal Martin's rusty old Ford Deluxe in front of her, but she couldn't think of a single reason why the man would be driving that direction, let alone the rest of the cars clogging the narrow road ahead of them.

"This is worse than the traffic to the fairgrounds at the start of summer! This *thing* really doesn't want us to get to Rebecca, huh?"

"I don't think it's so much that it wants Rebecca,"

Shirley said. "It just wants all the chaos that's happening around here right now. It's like it's hungry for it. Hungry for the sins of Raventree Hollow."

"Well, it's about to be quite disappointed." Katrina shifted gears, guided the car onto the shoulder, and left the cars idling on the road behind in a cloud of dust.

After a few more bends, they arrived at the turnoff that led up the western hill. The suspension groaned painfully as the coupe bounced over bumps and slammed into ditches in the steep, unpaved path. After a while, there seemed to be more mud than rain on the windows, and then the tires finally found a stretch of slippery road that the treads couldn't grip.

"We'll have to go the rest of the way on foot," Kat said. She looked down at her feet. "I'm glad I didn't wear my pumps, but these flats are certainly not going to survive our climb."

"Mother's going to ask why I didn't wear my galoshes," Shirley said as she lifted her feet to reveal her own flats. They looked at each other and laughed. Katrina was glad they could find joy amid the unexpected craziness of the day. She cut the engine, reached over to the glove compartment above Shirley's knees, and pulled out a flashlight.

They didn't have far to trek, though after each woman slipped two or three times, they were covered in more muck than they should have been from such a brief journey. The gates loomed large above them at the end of the path. Kat gave a tug and a push, but as she expected, they didn't budge.

"When was the last time you climbed a tree?" Shirley asked. She pointed to one that grew just feet from the wall with hearty branches that stretched over the other side. The tree split and stretched at an angle that looked easy enough to navigate.

"If I really were the witch everyone in town says I am, I could just zip over this wall on my broom, but the tree looks sturdy enough to support us." Kat walked past Shirley, as if eager to impress her young new friend, and started to climb.

"It's a good thing I'm with you and not Herman," Shirley quipped. "He's so uncoordinated, he'd likely fall right off and take me down with him."

"That boy?" Kat turned and smiled down at her. "He's so into you, I'd be surprised if he wasn't climbing a tree to stare into your window every night. I've seen the way he looks at you. Everybody in town has."

"I'm on the first floor, so he wouldn't have to climb far," Shirley said. "Besides, I kind of like someone else. I think Herman knows. At least, I hope he does." Kat saw confusion on the girl's face; perhaps she had just realized that she had grown more fond of Herman than she thought possible.

"That's the thing about love, Shirley." Kat climbed

the trunk of the tree until she was level with the top of the wall. She pushed down on the branch that extended to the wall; it seemed like it would hold her weight as she made her way over. "Even when everyone else says it's wrong, sometimes our hearts just won't take no for an answer."

The wall was wide enough to sit on, so Kat shifted off of the branch and onto the ancient stone structure, which was more supportive. On the other side of the wall, there was a mound of gravel that the nuns or their groundskeeper—if there was such a person in this strange old place—must have shoveled onto the driveway to fill ruts when needed.

"We'll have to drop down carefully. It's a bit of a shorter drop on this side, but it looks uneven." Kat gripped the rough stones that topped the wall and lowered herself down. Shirley did the same without trouble. "I've spent more than forty years of my life in this town, and I never thought I'd be inside these walls. This convent has loomed over the town and haunted our nightmares. I've had no desire ever to come here."

There was a sound almost like a waterfall ahead. Katrina and Shirley looked up and across the courtyard to see rainwater pouring down from the turrets high above. That's when they really took in the enormity of the place.

It was no mere convent. It stood like a sentry on

the top of the hill, watching over the town below. No, it was more of a predator, ready to consume them. It did not look like it could have been built in the relatively short lifespan of the country in which it resided; it would've been more at home in the Dark Ages. The stone walls looked ancient, but like so many antique structures of the Old World, it had somehow held together better than the wood-and-stucco or brick buildings of Raventree Hollow or any other place Kat had visited nearby. It had been built to last. To survive attacks and intruders. To repel unwanted visitors. And, perhaps, to hide the evil that lived within.

"It's like Count Dracula's castle," Shirley said. She took a step forward but stopped when Katrina shot out a hand.

"Please, Shirley, let's go back. We shouldn't be here. Don't you feel it?"

The younger woman turned and looked Kat in the eyes with full confidence. "I absolutely feel it. It doesn't want us here. That's how I know we must go in and help Rebecca."

She turned and moved toward the towering monstrosity. Katrina followed.

Chapter Twenty-Two

The warmth of Kenneth Chou's bare flesh against hers was *everything* to Alexandra. She basked in the euphoria of his presence anytime they were together. It was a feeling as incredible as what she had felt in the Japanese Gardens in the city. He filled her with clear-headedness and absolute pleasure.

The bed on which the two of them lay, however, was not at all pleasurable. The springs of the pull-out sofa bed dug into her more than the good doctor's flexing member, and she decided she couldn't take it anymore. Kenneth snorted hideously in his sleep as Alexandra rolled away from him and pulled herself up out of the sagging love nest they had made.

She much preferred making love on the exam table, the desk, the waiting room furniture—

anywhere but the couch in Kenneth's office. But Kenneth didn't feel right about any of that. He had paid a couple of young men to move this piece of furniture here from his home so the couple could engage in their forbidden romance away from either of their houses. Alexandra and Kenneth had made the sagging couch their own personal spot of sin and pleasure, and that was where Alexandra dozed off uncomfortably several evenings per week.

She watched him dream as she pulled her clothes back on and patted her hair into an acceptable position. He smiled in his sleep, and it would have been quite cute if not for the drool dribbling down his lip and onto the pillow. She thought about how wonderful a life of marriage to Kenneth would be, if not for the small-town minds that would judge her for marrying the Asian doctor. Alexandra was quite sure they were already whispering about the couple. The looks she received around town were not just pity for what had happened to her garden. It was more than that. They were *knowing* looks, mocking, scornful. But she was certain there was also jealousy. The doctor was young, muscular, and handsome, even despite the xenophobic standards of most of the townsfolk.

Screw them, Alexandra thought. *Kenneth Chou is more man than anyone in this town. He loves me. I love him. Nothing will get in the way of that.*

Nothing, that is, except perhaps the law.

The law would not be kind to her if the little man she had hired to take out the coach was sloppy and left evidence that tied back to her.

Alexandra picked through her purse and found the slip of paper with the phone number and the phony name Bard. She rushed out to the receptionist's desk and dialed the number. It rang once. Twice. Thrice.

A click.

"Who's this?" came a woman's voice. It was rough and full of suspicion. Alexandra hesitated. "I said, who is this?"

"Oh, um, I think I dialed the wrong number."

"If you're looking for that little putz Danny Bardino, you have the right number. He's just not here."

Bardino—it sounded close. "Yes, that's him," Alexandra said. "It's quite urgent. Do you know where I can find him?"

The woman let out a hacking cough and then spat quite audibly. "Danny's out on a research assignment. A more jealous person might think he's out with another woman, but I don't know if you've *seen* Danny. No worries there. No woman would be as dumb as I was, getting hitched to that dolt."

"Well, do you happen to know where he is? Can I reach him at a hotel?"

"He took the train west. Raventree Hollow, was it? Said he'd be back by morning, so he didn't go too far. What do you want with him, anyway? Is he in some kind of trouble again? Just wait until my father hears about whatever it is. He warned me. Cut me off, as if a writer could afford to pay the bills—"

"Writer? Um, yes. This is about his assignment. You've been quite helpful. Thank you."

Alexandra hung the phone up as the woman on the other end launched into another wet coughing fit. She took one last glance down the hallway toward Kenneth's office. He still seemed to be deep in slumber. She only hoped he would wake up and straighten the room before his receptionist arrived in the morning. Otherwise, the rumors would kick into overdrive.

Let them talk, she thought. *Once I clear up this situation with Bard, Kenneth and I can leave this town behind and start a new life somewhere else.*

She exited through the front door of Kenneth's medical practice, pulling the door shut behind her. Nancy and Olin Halloran were walking their fluffy white poodle down the sidewalk. The old woman gasped at the sight of Alexandra leaving the dark office of Doctor Chou, but her husband pulled her along.

"Good evening," Alexandra called after them. Olin nodded but did not address her. He pulled his umbrella low over his wife's head, and the pair increased their pace.

Alexandra opened her own umbrella and smiled.

<hr>

FOR A HIGH SCHOOL GYM TEACHER AND FOOTBALL coach, Alexandra had always thought there was something amiss about Willy Franklin's house. She didn't think the district paid the man enough for him to afford such an upscale home on Emerald Hill Place. All the other teachers she knew of hung up their hats in places like the Elm Heights apartment complex on the north side. The Emerald Hill neighborhood was where the town's doctors, dentists, bank owners, and the big-city commuters lived; Kenneth's abode was across the street and four doors down. Yet there was Coach Franklin's house, with a garden that was, she had to admit, kept up beautifully by Judy Franklin. Most of the lush plants had started life in Alexandra's own nursery.

She was just about to cross the street when the gunshots rang out. Two of them.

I'm too late, she thought.

Alexandra darted toward the house, splashing through the puddle at the curb. With every step, visions flashed through her mind of her dainty wrists in handcuffs, the shaming glares of her fellow citizens as they watched her trial in the local courthouse, and newspaper headlines pronouncing her the mastermind of murder.

I should be running the other way, not right into the crime scene, she thought, but her feet continued to carry her toward the coach's home.

As Alexandra approached the steps to the porch, the front door flew open and Judy ran toward her, screaming. She was in a fluffy purple robe, her hair in curlers, her hands over her ears. *The gunshots must have done a number on her eardrums*, Alexandra thought. Judy ran right past her as if not even noticing the late-night caller. Alexandra turned and watched her dart toward the sidewalk. All around them, bedroom lights flickered on and illuminated the otherwise darkened houses.

Another scream rang out, this one from inside the coach's house. Alexandra dropped her umbrella on the porch, stepped through the doorway, and looked around. Display cases lined both sides of the foyer, filled with trophies, medals, and sports memorabilia. Pictures of Willy outnumbered shots of his wife five-to-one. Alexandra had to admit that the man *was* quite handsome for the beefy athletic type, but even so, the display of vanity was overkill.

She followed the commotion up the stairs. As she neared the second-floor landing, someone was pushed out of a bedroom doorway. The man crashed into a bookshelf in the upstairs loft and took down a couple of shelves as he collapsed. The *g* through *l* volumes of an encyclopedia fell to the ground with the man, covering his face, but Alexandra still recognized his flabby little body.

"What the hell are you doing here?"

Alexandra turned to the bedroom doorway. Coach Franklin stood there in nothing but his little white briefs, fists clenched, sweat dripping from his forehead. There was no blood on his finely sculpted body—at least, none that looked like his own. Alexandra flushed with relief.

"I was walking past when I heard gunshots. Your wife came out the front door screaming hysterically, so I wanted to see if you were okay." She made a show of looking at the man on the ground with confusion. "Who in the world is this man?"

"Some second-rate burglar. Had a gun but didn't know how to use it. He fired two rounds into my ceiling when I tackled him. He was no match for these guns," the coach said, patting his own arms. In any other situation, Alexandra would have laughed.

Danny Bardino wept underneath the stack of encyclopedias but did not try to get up. He was mumbling something through his sobs—"Just a mistake, an accident, didn't mean to hurt anyone," she thought it was. The coach walked over and effortlessly pulled him by his loafers. As the hardcovers slid off of Danny's face, the would-be killer caught sight of Alexandra. His eyebrows lifted with recognition, even hope.

"You! P-please h-help me!" Blood caked what teeth remained in his mouth.

As the coach raised a fist toward the man, Alexandra quickly turned away and headed back down the stairs. She could hear the siren of Sheriff Holman's cruiser approaching. It was time to get out before she had to answer any questions about her presence in that neighborhood.

"Glad you're okay, Coach! Sounds like help is on the way."

"Ms. Pennington," Coach Franklin called when she had descended the first few steps. She turned and looked up through the banister at him. "I'm sorry my varsity team caused a ruckus in your yard. I've been making them run extra laps at practice every day since."

"Oh, it's no trouble. None at all."

Alexandra ran down the stairs and out of the house. She grabbed her umbrella and stepped through the crowd that had gathered in the street. A dozen neighbors stood around Judy, consoling her, while the flashing red-and-blue lights approached. Nobody paid any mind to Alexandra.

She was half a block from her home on Main Street when she heard another woman crying. Ronnie

Marie Jennings was sitting on the red-and-white-striped bench in front of Cooper's Castle of Confectioneries, head slumped toward her lap, her body convulsing with sobs and shivers.

"Ronnie Marie? You're soaking wet! Let's get you out of the rain." Alexandra held out a hand. Ronnie Marie looked up at her with red eyes, an odd look on her face. *Is it fear?* Alexandra wondered. "What's the matter? Why are you looking at me like that? Did someone hurt you?"

"No," Ronnie Marie managed to get out before resuming her crying session. She flung herself off the bench and threw her arms around Alexandra. After wailing like a baby for several more seconds, she finally composed herself enough to speak. "Oh, Alexandra, I'm so sorry. Please don't hate me for this."

"For what?" Alexandra asked. She gently pulled back from the unexpected embrace. "What's wrong?"

"I know something. I know what happened to your yard."

"Yes, I assume the whole town knows my garden was destroyed. You don't need to apologize, though."

"No, I don't just know it was destroyed. I know who did it."

"The team, yes. Coach Franklin just apologized to me, as a matter of fact."

"Not the first time. I mean the time it was *really* destroyed. Agnes Butterfield did it."

Despite the rain, Alexandra dropped her umbrella in shock. The cool water was not enough to temper the heat rising in her.

"She *what*? Agnes Butterfield was responsible for that?"

"Yes, but there's more," Ronnie Marie said. "There's something wrong with her. Something is wrong in her head. She—"

Ronnie Marie cut off with a gasp. Her eyes widened with sudden fear. Alexandra knew it was the look of rage on her own face that had scared the woman. Ronnie Marie took a quick step away and fell back onto the soaked bench.

"Don't hurt her," Ronnie Marie said. "Please don't. There really is something wrong with her."

"She tried to hurt me. My livelihood. My home. I'm going to make her pay for what she did." Alexandra turned, kicked her umbrella into the road, and stomped off toward the other end of Main Street, where the Raventree Inn stood in waiting.

Chapter Twenty-Three

"That girl. That rat bastard little girl. We'll kill her. We'll ravage and destroy her tonight. She and that Givens witch must die."

There was a sound of bones cracking. It was unnatural. Then a deep, inhuman grunting. The voice both belonged to the woman and was not at all of this world. Glass crunched under her feet. The stench of booze and gasoline would have stung her nostrils, had her earthly senses been working.

"Shirley Bettencourt must *die*!"

A floorboard creaked at the other end of the dark hall. A match flickered. The part of her that was still Agnes Butterfield recognized the face that was faintly visible in the tiny bit of light.

"Alexandra Pennington," she said, her natural

voice returning.

"Are those your final words?" Alexandra said before dropping the match.

The flames that arose gave Agnes a better view of the room. Two overturned gas cans, which had apparently been emptied all around the ground floor of the inn, lay next to the town's one-time premier flower merchant. When the cans ran dry, Alexandra had apparently raided Agnes's robust collection of whiskey and other spirits; broken bottles lined the edges of the hall where they had smashed against the walls. "Goodbye, Agnes."

Alexandra opened the front door, stepped into the night, and pulled the door closed behind her.

Before the smoke reached her nose, Agnes realized there was another stench coming from her: booze. She was soaked in it. *She wants to torch me along with my house*, Agnes realized. Anger rose in her. It went beyond her own capacity for rage; most of it belonged to whatever was sharing her consciousness. The thing that had been with her for quite some time. The evil that had possessed her.

A blood-curdling scream left her lips as the flames rapidly snaked through the hallway and up the walls. Despite the fall down the stairs earlier in the summer and the tumble she had taken from the second-floor balcony earlier in the day—glimpses of that confrontation were returning to her now—Agnes sped down the hallway. Her bones crunched, but she felt no pain. The flames greedily licked at her tattered, alcohol-soaked gown, but she paid them no mind either. She didn't even stop for the door. Agnes plowed through, sending splinters of wood everywhere. She took three steps to the edge of the porch and hurled her ample body into the air like a flaming cannonball.

Alexandra turned halfway around, shocked by the sudden agility of the recently disabled woman. They both collapsed into the street and rolled over each other one, two, three times before stopping in the middle of the pavement. They both lay there, stunned for a brief second, before Agnes felt herself get to her knees. She straddled Alexandra and started punching her in the face. Left cheek. Right cheek. Alexandra kicked and flailed, but Agnes was too heavy.

Despite the rain, Agnes suddenly realized how hot she felt. That was when she regained feeling in her body, at least momentarily. She looked down at herself and finally noticed she was still on fire. She let out a yelp, lunged to her right, and rolled around on the ground until the flames faded away.

"We hate her," she heard herself say, though she hadn't meant to. "We'll kill her!"

She looked to the curb, where the neighbor's trash can stood, awaiting the weekly municipal waste pickup. Without a thought for the weight of the full receptacle, she lifted it over her head and brought it down on top of Alexandra. It landed on the prone woman and rolled off. Agnes moved to pick it up when she noticed a flash of headlights and the screech of brakes.

It was too late.

The front end of the car connected with her body. She flew fifteen feet, landed in the street, and rolled another ten feet.

Through the blood in her eyes, she saw the car door open. A man jumped out.

"Oh my God!" he yelled in a panic. No, not a man —not quite. Practically a boy. He was gangly. Lanky.

Herman Stanley, her mind told its companion. Before she knew what she was doing, she was back on her feet, racing toward him, blocking out the pain of her many broken bones. She bowled into him, sending him down hard into the street. The passenger door opened, and this time the man who stepped out actually was of an age. *The good Pastor Laurence Wolfram*, she informed herself.

Agnes jumped into the car. The engine was still running. She put it into gear. Laurence barely dove out of the way before she sped off. She turned left onto Camellia Drive at the next intersection and took off toward the hills on the northwest side of town.

Chapter Twenty-Four

Perhaps *we could have avoided this entire situation if Sheriff Holman had just believed me,* Laurence thought. He looked around at the scene in disbelief.

The Raventree Inn had stood for more than seventy-five years, starting small and growing and modernizing as needed until it had fallen into disrepair when Agnes Butterfield's husband abandoned her. It was mostly Victorian, but various expansions had added bits of Craftsman style. Laurence's own grandfather and uncles had been part of the construction crews that had assembled bits and pieces of it over the years. Now it was in flames.

Alexandra Pennington lay sprawled out in the middle of the street, her face swollen and purple, a steady stream of blood coming out of her broken nose and split lip. Herman Stanley hunched over her, attempting to shield her from the rain while gently cushioning her head with his coat.

After leaving Rebecca Abrams with the Sisters of Mercy earlier that day, Laurence had gone straight to Sheriff Holman's office to report what had happened and what he feared was to come. The office was full of townsfolk, all there to report suspicious behavior by their friends, families, or neighbors. Even with his standing as the town's religious leader, Laurence waited for nearly three hours before being led into the sheriff's back office.

"So, let me get this straight," Sheriff Holman said, the disbelief in his eyes more mocking than surprised. "You greeted Ms. Abrams as she got off the train. You told her she was in danger, that she needed to go hide out with an order of reclusive penguins up in that creepshow of a convent while you took care of the mess. She went with you—willingly, I might add, so you don't come off as a kidnapper here—and now she's just hanging out with those old loons up there?"

"Yes, that's about right," Laurence said. "Though the nuns aren't as creepy as you think. They paid me a visit the other night. They clearly knew what was happening here in town, and they practically invited me to bring the girl to them for her own protection."

"And why didn't you just take her to her well-to-do fiancé's manor? You think he has something to do with this conspiracy with the innkeeper and the barber and the banker and half the others in this town?"

"No, that's not it." Laurence actually had no idea why he hadn't done that. It would have been the most sensible course of action, after all. "There was something else. Some kind of pull, like I was being made to take her there."

"Oh, so now God is involved in this, Pastor? Have you been sneaking a bit too much of that communion wine back in the sacristy?"

"Not at all, Sheriff. I don't know that what has been happening is *of God* at all. There is something sinister at play in this town. The nuns have been trying to warn me about it. It's like they're trying to protect us from evil, but that very evil is coming from where they live."

"So you took her right into the belly of the beast, then? Gotcha."

Laurence glanced across the desk at the pad of paper the sheriff had been scribbling on during their conversation. The man had written and crossed out several points Laurence had tried to make. Nothing had stuck.

"I'm sorry, Sheriff. I don't know how to make you believe me except to tell you to open your eyes and look around. Why is the lobby so full? Why has the dispatch phone been ringing off the hook the last couple of hours? Something is not right here at all."

"Well, I can look into the kidnapping plot you say Agnes Butterfield got you tangled up in. But I will not interfere with the Sisters of Mercy. They've been independent up there for as long as I've been alive, and I'm not looking to change that. Why don't you pick up the girl, deliver her to her fiancé, and then go back home and get some sleep? If you're truly scared of the old innkeeper, lock your doors tonight."

The sheriff rose with a sneer on his face. On cue, the door flew open. Constance Heffley, the evening dispatcher, was standing in the doorway with an alarmed expression.

"Reports of gunfire on Emerald Hill Place. Neighbors say Judy Franklin ran out of her house screaming something about a burglar."

Sheriff Holman lifted an eyebrow at Laurence. "If you'll excuse me, I have some more evil to vanquish in my town," he said as he grabbed his leather coat off the rack and slipped on his peaked cap.

Laurence, ashamed by his own actions and his inability to convince the sheriff of the danger the town was in, walked back into the lobby with his head down. The standing-room-only crowd called for the lawman's attention, but Holman sped past them without a word, rushing out the door and into his cruiser, which was parked just out front. Someone grabbed Laurence's shoulder, spun him around, and pushed him into the wall. A few people in the room gasped or silenced their desperate chatter.

"Where's Shirley?" Herman Stanley asked, his elbow and forearm pressed across Laurence's chest to pin the older man against the wall. There was a younger boy with Herman, the awkward kid who volunteered at the library. "You knew she was on to you, so you grabbed her outside the library, didn't you? I found my car keys on the sidewalk. She wouldn't have dropped them there unless she was being taken and wanted me to find them. Is Sheriff Holman in on it, too? Is that why you're here?"

Laurence wanted to choose his words carefully. There were two dozen pairs of eyes on him, and his reputation as an even-minded moral leader of the town was on the line. All he'd ever wanted was to develop and strengthen the faith of every soul in Raventree Hollow. To do so, he'd built relationships with people of all generations, greeted each person by name when he passed them on the street or stood in line with them at the market. He'd refrained from social engagements and relationships that could jeopardize his standing. And now he'd put all of that at risk to take part in Agnes's rumormongering and scheming. In that lobby, he had one last chance to denounce evil, to set himself apart, to show the people that he would live up to his role and reputation. If they saw his faith as a facade, as phoniness, then their own faith would be diminished. Such was the job of a clergyman: a mere mortal like everyone else, confronted with the same temptations but called upon to stand above it all.

"No," Laurence gasped. "Please, you must believe me. The sheriff didn't listen to a word I said. I know nothing about Shirley, but I can guess who—or *what* —has her. The library isn't far from Agnes's place. She seems to be at the center of all this."

It took some more work to convince Herman that Laurence had only been pretending to play along because he knew something evil had overtaken Agnes, but he eventually won Herman over. With the sheriff gone, several people in the room suddenly began to see Laurence as the authority figure. They rushed over to him with their concerns and complaints, and soon he was pinned against the wall not by Herman's lanky arm but by their desperation. As he did his best to repair his reputation with the people, he felt a piercing glance from Arnie McCann, but the boy never once spoke to him.

By the time Laurence managed to slip outside, Herman was sitting in the Stanley family sedan, idling in the spot normally reserved for Sheriff Holman's cruiser. Herman leaned across the passenger seat and popped open the door for Laurence. He got in and pulled the door shut, catching one last glimpse of

Arnie staring out from the doorway of the sheriff's office. Then Herman released the brake and sped toward the opposite side of Main Street.

It was at the far end of Main that Herman's headlights shone on Agnes savagely beating a female figure they both assumed was poor Shirley Bettencourt. When Herman made no move to slow down, Laurence grabbed the boy's arm and called for him to stop. Herman ignored the plea and plowed right into the innkeeper. She got right up as if she'd merely taken a little tumble, then rushed to the car they'd exited and sped away, nearly taking off Laurence's toes, muttering something about needing to kill the witch and the Bettencourt girl.

And now here they were. The woman in the street was not Shirley at all but Alexandra Pennington. The flames from the inn cast a terrifying light over the bloody woman. Yet through the blood and tears on her face, Laurence saw something in her eyes. Something pure evil. The same thing he'd seen in Agnes. And despite the woman's obvious injuries, Alexandra Pennington sat up, got to her feet, and teetered away down the street.

"Ms. Pennington, wait!" Laurence called after her. She turned toward them and let out an inhuman growl. Then she resumed her trek in the same direction Agnes had sped off in moments earlier.

A pair of headlights illuminated Alexandra as a

pickup turned onto Main from Camellia. Unlike Herman, the driver didn't try to run down the pedestrian. Benjamin White slammed on his brakes, skidded several feet, and came to a halt just a foot away from Alexandra. He opened the door to his truck and stepped out.

"Jesus, lady, what the hell are you doing in the street? Wait, Alexandra, is that you?"

Laurence watched in shock as Alexandra charged the man and tackled him to the pavement as effectively as one of the players on the varsity team. She quickly got back to her feet, jumped into the pickup, and threw it in reverse before even bothering to close the door. She sped off.

Laurence made to run over to the injured newcomer, but Herman grabbed his arm and spun him around.

"Someone's coming," the younger man said.

Sure enough, another car was approaching from behind them with its headlights off. The car was cruising unsteadily—accelerating, then braking, veering from side to side. Laurence and Herman watched in awe as the car swerved to the right, crashed into the picket fence across the street from the burning inn, and came to a halt. The driver's side window rolled down.

"Get in," a boy said from inside, calm and

collected. Herman walked toward the car, and Laurence followed.

"Arnie!" Herman cried out. He jumped into the front passenger seat without question. "Boy, are we glad to see you! Where'd you get the ride?"

"Stole it. Sheriff Holman's personal car. Leaves the keys right on his desk."

Well, I suppose nothing should surprise me about tonight, Laurence thought.

As he climbed into the back seat, he spotted a shotgun resting on the dashboard.

Okay, almost nothing.

Chapter Twenty-Five

Shirley didn't dare use the oversize front doors. The inhabitants of the castle-turned-convent would likely be waiting just inside, expecting Laurence or someone else involved in his little conspiracy to return for the captive Rebecca. She turned toward the east side of the property but halted when she caught sight of the massive tower that perched at the edge of the hill, intimidating the town below. Though she had heard its resounding bell ringing every day of her life and never thought twice about it, something about the tower now filled her with dread. When she turned away from it, she saw the same fear on Katrina's face that she knew must be apparent on her own. She changed course and led Katrina to the west end of the castle instead. Around the corner, they found a smaller door made of heavy wood that had been battered over the years by inclement weather. A peek through the window a foot away revealed an empty mudroom. Shirley nodded to Katrina.

"It might be locked," the older woman said. Her hand trembled on the rusted doorknob, unable to get a proper grip. Shirley reached out her own hand and set it gently on Katrina's.

"Most everyone in town leaves their doors unlocked every night. Up here behind this protective wall, I really doubt they bother to lock theirs. We'll do it together."

Shirley felt Katrina's hand still. Katrina whispered, "Right, then," and the two women turned the knob together. There was a grittiness to it from the rust; it felt like the metal was catching on sandpaper as it turned. When it had rotated all the way clockwise, Shirley expected the door to swing inward, but it remained stuck in place. Shirley and Katrina simultaneously put their shoulders against the door and pushed their combined weight into it. It groaned on ancient hinges, and a combination of wood dust and paint chips sprinkled down from the edges of the frame.

They stepped inside, greeted by a wave of mildew stench. Shirley looked down to find that the stone floor was covered in a damp green layer of moss and sludge. Rainwater was pooling along one wall, apparently seeping in through a gap between the wall and floor. She pushed the door closed behind her, but it no longer seemed to fit properly in the warped frame. Candles burned in sconces along the wall, highlighting the apparent lack of electricity in the castle. Shirley was relieved that Katrina had brought the flashlight from her car.

They heard no sign of life, so they made their way deeper into the building. On the other side of the next door, they found themselves in a pantry. "This is larger than my kitchen at home," Katrina quipped. She checked one door, but it only led to a descending flight of stairs. "Probably the root cellar," she guessed. Across the pantry was a larger door, so they went through it. As Shirley expected, it led to a kitchen. There were no modern appliances. The last dying embers in an oversize fireplace smoked lazily, an ancient iron pot hanging on a hook above.

"Looks like we missed supper," Shirley joked. The surfaces were spotless, scrubbed clean after the meal. It was a marked difference from the soggy mudroom.

There was a door just to Shirley's left and one straight across the room from her, both shut tight. Katrina moved to the far side of the kitchen and tried that door, the larger of the two. She opened it just a couple of inches so she could peer through with one eye. She closed it gently and moved back toward

Shirley. "A hallway. I think the first room off the hall is the dining room. No sign of life."

Shirley checked the door nearest her. It led to a narrow stairwell that rose into darkness. No sconces lit the steep corridor. "This was probably the servants' staircase," she said. "I have a feeling we'll find Rebecca up there."

"Good enough for me." Katrina flicked on the flashlight and started up the stairs ahead of Shirley. They were wooden, and a strip of worn burgundy carpet ran down the middle of them, leaving six inches of exposed wood on either side. Four steps up, Shirley noticed the wood bow under Katrina's foot, and the groan of it echoed through the enclosed corridor. Shirley avoided that step as she climbed behind Katrina.

At the top, they went through another narrow door. They were in a small sitting room in what would have been the servants' wing. It may as well have been a cave; wax crept down the walls from sconces and dried into stalactites, while the candles on the tables were like stalagmites, piercing up into the dank, dark air.

Shirley walked over to a stack of leather-bound books on a table and flipped through them. The top one was in Latin, the next in English. Both were Bibles seemingly as ancient as the castle. She set them aside and looked at the third book down. There was no cross adorning the cover. Embossed on the front was a series of symbols: a leaf, an eye, a serpent, a sun, a flame, a crescent moon, a goat's head. *What does it mean?* she wondered. As she lifted the cover, Katrina snapped her fingers from across the room. Shirley looked over at her and nodded. She set the first two books back on the stack and crossed to her companion.

They moved down a hallway, opening each door as quietly as they could. These doors moved easily enough, and from the looks of the rooms beyond, they were used regularly as the Sisters of Mercy's bedrooms. Each held three beds. In two rooms, they could hear the breathing of heavy sleepers, including one particularly egregious snorer. These doors they did not open, but the stench of sickness seeped under the last door they passed along with the snores. Shirley's foot connected with something, and she tumbled over. She looked back to see Katrina righting a chamber pot, liquid sloshing slightly over the edge in the direction Shirley had fallen. They looked at each other in disgust. Katrina checked her hands, but they were mercifully clean. Shirley got to her feet, and they resumed.

The hall ended in a door, which they passed through. Another hall lay beyond, this one grander and clearly intended for the original residents of the house. A banister ran along the right side, overlooking a dark foyer below. There were candles lit down there, but their sheen didn't extend beyond a few inches each.

The limited illumination below darkened, then returned a moment later. Someone—or some*thing*—had gone past the candles. Shirley's heart jumped. She grabbed Katrina's sleeve. The woman took her hand to calm her. They moved away from the banister and continued down the hall. A narrow door appeared along the wall to their left. They opened it, walked through, and found themselves surrounded by heavy curtains on three sides. Shirley peeled back a curtain from one corner, then quickly reached back to pull Katrina forward.

They were on a balcony overlooking a chapel that rivaled Laurence's sanctuary in the town below. In between several of the pews, nuns knelt, their heads bowed in prayer. The faint, breathy whispers of the women reached Shirley and Katrina, but they couldn't make out any individual words. Shirley still saw no sign of Rebecca. They carefully backed out into the hall. It continued past the main stairway and down another dark corridor, though there seemed to be no more candles in that direction.

"That must lead to what was once the family's suites," Katrina whispered. "Probably abandoned for decades now."

Next to the landing of the main stairs, there was

another flight that led up to the third floor. Along the wall to the left of those stairs, candles burned. Shirley pointed, and they both headed in that direction. As they neared the staircase, Shirley noted that the candles were much more well-tended than the others. There were no aggregated layers of wax drippings. They'd apparently been burning for mere hours rather than days or weeks.

"I think we're on the right track," Shirley whispered.

They made their ascent. The air grew warmer as they reached the top, but it wasn't as pleasant as Shirley had hoped. It was heavy with humidity, the stench of mold overwhelming. She swallowed down an impending cough, but her eyes watered and her sinuses flared. At the top, the hallway was much narrower than the one on the second floor. Water dripped from a crack in the ceiling and pooled in the soggy carpet. Their feet made sloshing sounds as Katrina and Shirley made their way to the first door.

Katrina turned the handle, and they both entered. Immediately to her left, Shirley noticed a hefty statue of Saint Nicholas set in a niche in the wall. To her right, there was an old crib, tilting sadly to one side where a leg had rotted and collapsed. A rat jumped out of what must have once been a baby's blanket and came right toward Shirley. She jumped aside as the creature brushed past her and out the door. It took all of her strength not to scream. Unfortunately, Katrina did the screaming for her.

It was actually more of a yelp, but it was the most noise they had made since entering the mudroom on the first floor. It was enough of a ruckus for someone to hear.

"Hello?" a confused voice said from farther down the hall. It wasn't the aged croak Shirley would have expected from the women of the cloth downstairs.

"That has to be Rebecca," Shirley whispered.

They went back into the hall, not bothering to close the nursery door behind them. Shirley reached the door before Katrina and reached for the handle. She took a deep breath. If she was wrong, they were compromised. She tightened her grip on the knob and turned.

It caught.

She turned counterclockwise, but it still wouldn't give.

"Of course it's locked," Shirley whispered. "What did I expect?"

"The key must be around here somewhere," Katrina said, no longer bothering to whisper. She shined the flashlight around at the walls, but there was no key hanging from a nail or hook, no shelves that held what they were looking for. Shirley reached up to the top of the door frame, hoping the key was resting there. No luck.

"I have an idea," Shirley said. She ran to the rat-infested nursery and reemerged a few seconds later cradling the statue of Saint Nicholas, patron saint of children and unmarried girls. She hammered the full weight of it down on the doorknob, which busted right off of the moist wood and dropped to the floor. Shirley set the statue down and pushed open the door. It was fully dark inside the room, but Katrina's flashlight illuminated the person within.

Rebecca Abrams was sitting on what had once been the governess's bed. The room had been swept and dusted. The linens had been changed. No rats jumped out of the dark corners.

"Who are you?" Rebecca asked. "And why did you smash that antique doorknob? I have the key right here. I would have just unlocked the door if you had knocked!"

"We're here to help get you back to Phillip," Shirley said. She felt her skin heating up slightly at the mention of his name. "I'm Shirley, and this is Katrina. I saw Pastor Laurence nab you and force you up here to this terrible castle."

"What?" Rebecca asked. "He didn't *nab* me. He told me I was in danger and he wanted to help."

"Why did you trust him? You don't even know him, right?" Shirley asked.

"I don't know him personally, no, but Phillip trusts him. He asked him to officiate our wedding.

We're planning to elope at the manor later this week!"

"He *what*?" Katrina spluttered out. "You mean Larry knew that you and Phillip were getting married? Since when?"

"Well, I believe Phillip called him just the other night. Since his family is no longer with us and my family is not very supportive of our union, we decided we wanted something small and quick. We've been apart all summer because I was traveling around Europe."

"He was just protecting you. I should have known!" Katrina turned to Shirley. "How could I ever have doubted him? Of course he wasn't in on it all along!"

"I'm so sorry I put doubt in your mind. That's my fault," Shirley said, hugging Katrina. "I just thought—"

A crash from outside cut Shirley off. All three women ran to the window and peered out. A car had plowed through the gate and was speeding across the courtyard out front.

"That's Herman's car!" Shirley shouted with excitement. It swerved recklessly through the yard and approached a large tree but didn't slow down. Shirley's voice grew horrified. "What is he doing?"

Herman's automobile slammed into the tree. As if in slow motion, a body burst through the windshield, hurtled through the air, and slammed down on the rocky pavement, rolling several feet before coming to a stop.

"That's not Herman," Katrina said.

The body twitched on the ground. The headlights shined on it like a spotlight illuminating a stage performer. Shirley saw it wasn't a man at all.

"Agnes?" Shirley uttered in shock. The convulsions seemed to have stopped, and all was still. "Is she dead?"

Agnes sat up abruptly. All three women screamed. As if the would-be corpse below had heard them, she peered directly up at their window. They all dropped to the floor.

"Who is that?" Rebecca asked.

"That's who we thought Laurence was working with," Shirley answered. "She's the one who wanted to make you disappear."

There was a cackle down below. Shirley rose slowly and peeked through the dust-caked glass. Agnes was now standing. Her left arm hung unnaturally crooked. Neither leg appeared straight, either. Blood was flowing out of a gash that ran along her right cheek. Yet despite all odds, Agnes took a step. And another. She walked out of the beam of the headlights and was lost to the darkness.

"I'm coming for you! The little bitch and the stupid witch! Phillip Winfield's wench as well. You're all dead!" The voice certainly came *from* Agnes Butterfield, but Shirley couldn't help but feel that the voice wasn't *of* Agnes Butterfield. The woman had always been highly unpleasant, but she had never been purely evil. *No*, Shirley thought, *something else is at play here, but what?*

The walking mess that was Agnes came into view once again as another pair of lights approached. "What now?" Katrina asked, popping up alongside Shirley to peer out the window. This time, it was a pickup truck that rumbled over the fallen gate and came to a halt next to Herman's car. The woman who jumped out was tall and slender, but her head hung to one side, apparently injured.

"Why, hello again, Alexandra," Agnes said. The two women ran toward each other at full speed. They collapsed together onto the cobblestone pathway and began throwing punches at each other.

That was enough for Shirley. "We have to get out of here while they're distracted," she said. She grabbed Rebecca's hand and made for the door with Katrina just behind them. They made it to the top of the staircase before Shirley heard footsteps coming up. She turned and led the women toward the east wing. "There must be another stairway on this side!"

Down the hall they went, around a couple of turns, plowing through spiderwebs every couple of feet. They heard footsteps behind them, struggling and failing to keep up. Around another bend, Shirley almost took a tumble down an unseen staircase, but Rebecca planted her feet and yanked her upright before she made the plunge.

"Thanks," Shirley said. She felt around for the railing, grabbed hold, and started her descent. They went down to the second-floor landing, took another turn, and made their way to the first floor.

They found themselves at the far eastern end of a hallway that seemed to stretch along the entire rear of the castle. There was only one more door beyond the stairs, flanked by two life-size statues of ancient knights in full armor, each holding a sword. Both the armor and the swords were tarnished with age and neglect. "Let's try that one. Maybe it leads out the back."

This door was different from the others. Whereas every other door they'd passed was a proper interior door, this one was made of heavy wood. Plates of iron were fitted over it as if to reinforce it from a formidable intruder. Above the doorknob, there were six bolts of various types and ages, all firmly locked. The three women started unfastening them, and when the last one clicked loudly under Shirley's hand, the door moved on its own.

Shirley braced for the warm, humid summer air to hit her. It never came.

Chapter Twenty-Six

The door didn't lead outside at all. Instead, the women found themselves in the bell tower.

It was frigid... unnaturally so. It didn't feel like a cold draft one might expect in an old stone structure. There wasn't a cool breeze cycling through the hollow cylindrical building. It was something else— an absence of warmth, perhaps, rather than the presence of coolness. But it was also more than that. The air felt foreign on Shirley's skin. Alien. Unearthly.

And the smell...

Breathing in the air in that place was like snorting something toxic that burned her nostrils, her throat, her lungs. It felt as if particles of something—sharp yet gelatinous—filled her with every breath, tearing up her insides and sticking like some kind of blobby, congealed sludge. And with each inhale, Shirley was certain she would retch from the stench. It was like the time her family had gone up to her grandfather's cabin in the mountains a few months after he passed away. The electrical company had shut off the power after the deceased man had failed to pay the bill. He hadn't *planned* to croak while visiting Shirley's family in Raventree Hollow, so his refrigerator had still been full of perishables. Shirley had tagged along with her father to clean out the cabin so they could sell the property, and she didn't think she'd ever forget the odor of that place. She was the one who had opened the icebox door. Inside, a discolored steak had crawled with maggots; spoiled eggs had unleashed a brutal scent. Mold as furry as a cat had spread over everything. Shirley's vomit had blended right in with the mess.

But this... this was worse by a long shot.

"There's no way out from here," Katrina said. "Let's go back the way we came."

"Wait," Shirley said. Something had caught her eye. "Give me your flashlight."

Katrina handed it over without argument. Shirley aimed it down to find a large wooden platform covering the center of the circular floor. The beam of light ran along one plank, then another, and another.

"There!" Shirley shouted. She held the beam still over a crack in the wood.

"It must be as ancient as the rest of this place," Rebecca said. "It's no surprise the wood is rotting away. What's the big deal?"

"No, there was something else. I just—"

A bubble protruded from the crack and popped.

"Is there something alive down there?" Katrina asked. Before another bubble came out, the women turned as a banging sound from somewhere back in the castle reached their ears. "I think Agnes and Alexandra have made it through the front doors."

Crazed laughter rang through the long halls, followed by a scream.

"I think we should take our chances with this room," Rebecca said, "bubbles or no bubbles. Let's go up those stairs!"

Shirley shone the light toward the staircase Rebecca was pointing at. The steps were splintered wood, and one was missing for every three or four that hung crookedly. She raised the light higher, noticing for the first time that a rope dangled down from unseen heights and ended just over the center of the wooden platform. Above, there were several landings as the staircase twisted around the circumference of the cylindrical tower.

It was impossibly tall.

"Did the tower look this big from the outside?" Katrina asked. "That's definitely taller than four stories! I've seen this place for decades from down below, and I *know* it shouldn't be this tall!"

Another psychotic cackle came from the dark hall of the castle. Shirley ran over and slammed the door shut. That was when she realized the locks were on the other side.

"The bench!" she shouted. She flashed her light at what appeared to be a pew from the castle's chapel. It sat awkwardly straight along one of the rounded walls. Together, the three women hoisted it up and wedged one end against the door.

They ran to the stairs. As Shirley expected, each board creaked loudly underfoot, ready to give up the ghost.

"At least the rail feels firm," Rebecca said. "Hold on tight."

They'd made it up to the first landing when they heard pounding at the door.

"Little Shirley Bettencourt, open up!" shouted a twisted version of Agnes Butterfield's voice. "I promise I'll make your death as slow and painful as possible. The same goes for that Givens witch you have with you."

The pounding got more intense, but the pew held its ground. Then Agnes stopped.

Shirley, Katrina, and Rebecca crouched on the second-floor landing, peering down into the darkness below. Their panting breaths were the only sounds in the tower. With the flashlight aimed to the side, Shirley could just make out the fear on her companions' faces.

Rebecca's face twisted slightly as if she was about to whisper something, but a new sound made her stay silent.

It was a gurgling sound, almost like a bubble of water echoing up through a jug, yet thicker. Muckier.

Shirley lowered the flashlight toward the wooden platform below. She counted five bubbles. Six. All in one particularly wide crack between the boards.

Then came the slamming.

Something massive was throwing quite a lot of weight against the platform from underneath. The whole thing buckled upward. Again and again, like tribal ritual drumming, the sounds came. With each hit, liquid splashed out from the cracks. Another hit, and an entire board splintered off like a toothpick. Shirley could now see just how thick the wood was; it was thicker than the railroad ties her father had used in their backyard to make a retaining wall for her mother's herb garden. Another board flew up, and the liquid sprayed as high as their platform. The smell, already nearly unbearable, grew even stronger.

Shirley wiped her face, then held her hand under the light. The liquid was a brownish green slimy sludge.

"Let's keep moving!" Rebecca said.

Shirley felt Rebecca grab her hand and let the woman pull her and Katrina up the next set of stairs. Six steps up, a board gave way under Shirley's feet, taking three lower steps down with it. Shirley's stomach leapt into her throat as she suddenly dropped. Rebecca tightened her grip on Shirley's left hand. Shirley involuntarily let go of the flashlight with her right and reached up for Katrina. As she dangled over the drop, she heard the flashlight hit a step on a lower level and roll down to the ground. The other two women pulled Shirley up as the entire wooden platform around them buckled and groaned. They made it to the next landing, and all three sat to catch their breath.

Shirley looked down at the ground. The flashlight miraculously seemed to be in one piece. It was perfectly aimed across the center of the room. Another bang sounded from below the platform, and this time Shirley saw what was causing the damage.

A tentacle as thick as a man's body protruded from the liquid and flailed about, shredding what remained of the wooden boards in the center of the room. Then a second one popped out of the muck as if to assist the first. They made quick work of the rest of the platform.

In the slim beam of the flashlight, one tentacle looked sickly grey, while the other was a green that almost matched the sludge that had splashed on Shirley moments earlier. As the green tentacle lobbed itself at the last of the splintered wood, the grey one stretched even farther toward the pew and the door. Its movements weren't controlled and stable but wobbly, drunken, clumsy. After swinging itself inches above the pew, it swooped downward and whacked the bench, which tipped over and slid across the floor like an empty can kicked by a child.

The light just reached the door, which Shirley watched open. Agnes Butterfield stepped through. The grey tentacle straightened up as if standing at attention. Agnes took another step into the light. Next to Shirley, Katrina gasped.

Shirley squinted through the dimness and saw what had shocked her: Agnes was dragging Alexandra Pennington into the tower by the hair. Once she was a few steps in, Agnes dropped Alexandra, whose head hit the ground hard. When the woman made contact with the floor, the green tentacle seemed to share in her pain. It slammed against the opposite wall and then retreated into the pit of liquid.

Agnes reached toward the grey tentacle. Its tip bent slightly like a head bowing in prayer. It moved slowly toward Agnes. She brushed her fingers against it, then her entire hand, as if petting a cute little puppy.

"You should not have come here," came a voice from the darkness. It was a woman's voice, haggard and tired. The speaker coughed as if it had hurt her to speak. She stepped through the doorway behind Agnes.

It was a nun. Behind her, several more nuns came through the door, large torches in hand, and made their way carefully around the edge of the circular room, stepping over the rubble from the destroyed platform. The room was suddenly full of light.

"You dare to speak?" Agnes asked. "I thought your tongues were cut out."

"One of us was chosen to remain whole so that we may pray against the resurrection of the beasts."

"Such good it did you," Agnes said. Her voice changed with each word. Her throat seemed to fill with saliva, and by the last word, she nearly gurgled. The liquid in the pit bubbled in unison. "Your entire lives were wasted, as were those who came before you, yet for me, it was but a night's rest."

Before the nun could respond, there was a new commotion. Alexandra shot up to her feet and threw all of her weight into Agnes's lower half. Agnes's legs buckled, and she fell toward the pit. The green tentacle shot out of the muck and tangled itself around the grey one. Agnes nearly toppled over the edge, but the wrestling beasts hit her like a golf club, and she flew into a nun along the wall. The grey tentacle escaped the green one's grip just long enough to turn back toward Alexandra. It flung itself toward her, too fast for her to get up from her hands and knees. It was centimeters away when a massive blast rang out and echoed through the tower.

Chapter Twenty-Seven

Shirley instinctively covered her head with her arms and closed her eyes. She opened them a second later when she felt Katrina rising to her feet inches away. She looked up at Katrina, then back down as another boom sounded.

Standing in the doorway was Arnie McCann. The kick of the shotgun had sent him flying back against the door, which hung open. The grey tentacle recoiled and trembled in apparent pain. Tarry black blood oozed out of two holes in the creature. The green tentacle, the nuns, Agnes, and Alexandra all remained frozen in shock.

Alexandra rose to her feet and took one step toward the boy. Behind her, the green tentacle flung itself in the same direction. Arnie started to pump the shotgun, but there wasn't enough time. The tentacle was just one foot away from ripping off Arnie's face when a tarnished sword swung out and sliced off the tip. Alexandra fell to the ground as if the sword had hit her instead. She cried out in pain. The green tentacle immediately pulled back, and the wielder of the sword stepped into the light.

"Herman!" Shirley yelled. He looked up at her and lifted the sword like a winning gladiator. In unison, everyone on the ground level looked up at the three women for the first time. It also served as a reminder of their presence to whatever beast deep within the pit commanded the tentacles.

The ground shook. The walls rumbled. Here and there, old stones broke away from the tower walls and plummeted to the bottom, some striking nuns, others splashing into the liquid of the pit. The green and grey tentacles stretched out and flailed wildly, swatting at everyone in the room. The grey one wrapped itself around a nun, who screamed incomprehensibly without her tongue and only quieted when she was pulled into the pit. The green tentacle swung at the first flight of stairs just as a fleeing nun attempted to make the climb. It shattered the entire set of steps, and the first landing came down as well, crushing two of the nuns while the climber lay at the very edge of the pit. Agnes walked over to the injured old woman and used her right foot to roll her into the darkness below.

Laurence ran through the doorway, where he'd been watching the scene in shock. He darted over to stop Agnes, but he was too late. He tackled her anyway, and they both fell just inches from the pit. They rolled over each other, away from the edge. Agnes wound up on top and began throwing punches at the pastor's face. She would have broken the man's nose and cheekbones had a nun not knocked her off of Laurence with a broken wooden step. Up on the third-floor landing, Katrina grabbed Shirley's arm.

"There must be something we can do," Katrina said.

Shirley looked around at the chaos. The broken stairs ensured they were trapped. The nuns were no match for the tentacles. Arnie was apparently out of ammunition. Herman stood in front of two injured nuns huddled against a wall, swinging the sword around any time the tentacles approached him. Everyone seemed to be doomed.

As Shirley looked at Arnie, his story came back to her. His grandmother had told him that the evil resided in this hill, that it caused death and destruction for anyone who tried to live here. Until, that is, they covered the pit.

Shirley looked up. The massive bell loomed over everyone at the very top of the tower, impossibly large. Its circumference was nearly as big as the tower's. It appeared to be perfectly centered, with only a few feet between its rim and the wall. Just like the pit below.

"Herman!" Shirley shouted. In the chaos, he didn't seem to hear her. Rebecca and Katrina joined in. "Herman! Up here!"

Herman looked up. Despite the surrounding madness, he flashed his goofy smile at Shirley.

"The sword! I need you to throw up the sword!" Shirley yelled. He looked at her, confused, then turned and ran through the doorway into the castle.

"Did he... did he just run away?" Rebecca asked in disbelief.

Herman reemerged a few seconds later with a second sword. He looked around and realized the lower flight of stairs was completely gone.

"What do I do?" he yelled.

Shirley looked down. Only half a flight of stairs remained on the way down to the second level, but the landing there was still intact. If she jumped down to it, though, she wouldn't be able to get back up.

"Only one of us needs to go down there," Rebecca said. "I'll do it. I'll retrieve the sword and toss it the rest of the way up."

Shirley looked up at the bell again. It hung from at least a dozen ropes that went up to the ceiling, through some anchored hoops, then down along the walls, where they were tied around hooks.

"We need both swords!" Shirley called down.

Herman nodded. She turned back to Rebecca. "Okay, grab both, then get as close to the wall as you can." She pointed to a window that was set into the wall on the lower level. It had a ledge that appeared just deep enough to sit on. "Try to get on the windowsill. Hold on as tight as you can."

Herman threw one sword up onto the landing. Shirley knew he had never been athletic. He'd never gone out for the football team, or even the basketball team, despite his height. He was too awkward and gangly. Yet his throw was perfect, as was the next. With the blades secure on the landing, Rebecca made her way down the remaining couple of steps. As she bent her knees slightly to make the jump down to the lower platform, the stairs rattled and cracked under her. She launched herself forward just as the wood crumbled beneath her feet, and she landed at the very edge of the platform.

Rebecca lay in shock for a few seconds until the wretched air of the tower returned to her lungs. Then she crawled over to the other end of the landing, where the two swords awaited her. She tossed them up to Shirley's platform one at a time. Shirley and Katrina each grabbed one and made their way carefully up the remaining flights of stairs.

Below, the chaos continued. The tentacles flailed, knocking over the surviving nuns and keeping them from fleeing. Arnie held the shotgun by the barrel, swinging it like a baseball bat anytime the tentacles came near him. Herman and Laurence huddled against a wall, watching Shirley and Katrina climb up the rickety stairs. Agnes and Alexandra had resumed their tussle, each using any debris she could lift to maim the other.

Up and up Shirley climbed with Katrina close at her heels. Near the top, the stench of the room cleared. Instead of the small glass-paned windows that lined the rest of the staircase, the openings near the bell were large and let in the outside air. The rain was still coming down. The wood at Shirley's feet was spongy from the elements. Moss grew everywhere. The ropes looked as old and frail as Shirley had expected.

"Stick as close to the edge as you can," she reminded Katrina, though she wasn't sure it would matter. She gripped the hilt of her sword with both hands, brought it up over her right shoulder, and slashed with all her strength at the rope in front of her. The blade sliced right through, and the wooden beams above the bell groaned.

"I don't like the sound of that," Katrina said before bringing her blade down through a rope on the other side. The whole tower quaked. With each rope they cut, the trembles grew.

"It's not just from us," Shirley said. She looked

down, realizing there was an unfamiliar noise coming from the bottom of the tower.

Out of the pit, three more tentacles appeared. One of them was much narrower than the others. It shot straight at the one nun who could still talk. She tried to jump out of the way, but it pierced through her left ear and shot out the right side before wrapping around her cranium. The nun screamed out in unimaginable pain, and then the noise turned into something fully inhuman, somewhere between an animalistic groan and demonic laughter.

"Sister Bernadette is a gluttonous cow!" the nun shouted in a deep, otherworldly voice. "She volunteers for kitchen duty every night so she can sneak extra portions!"

The tower rumbled. Another tentacle came out of the muck. The nun's arms moved to block it, but there wasn't enough strength left in her. The tentacle gripped her, and Shirley heard the snapping of bones all the way from the topmost level. Even in death, the voice continued to emanate from the nun's body.

"Sister Hailey keeps a stash of filthy adulterous books under her bed. She got them from Father Granthorne when he still presided over us. Their affair drove him away!"

Another quake.

Another tentacle.

The tremors were too much for the old tower.

The platform just one level below Shirley collapsed and plummeted down, headed right for Rebecca. The would-be bride saw it coming and was quick to act. She darted across what remained of her platform, leapt toward the center of the room, and grabbed hold of the rope that dangled all the way down from the center of the bell. Her aim was spot-on, but her strength failed her. She lost her grip and fell downward. One of the larger tentacles, this one a greenish blue, was swinging in an arc on its way to swatting Arnie. It hit her instead, and she flew across the room, landing next to Laurence and Herman. She was clearly hurt, but it sure beat being dragged down into the muck by the tentacles.

A gurgling, suckling sound came from the pit. The tremors grew stronger. The stone floor along the perimeter of the room began to crack.

A head emerged. It wasn't as large as the pit itself, which allowed room for the tentacles to continue their erratic movements. Its color was an amalgam of all the tentacles, like a disturbed satanic rainbow. There were rows of eyes all around the thing. It didn't appear to have a mouth at first, but slits opened up when it let out a screeching groan.

Everyone stopped moving. All the tentacles rose up and arced, but they too froze in place in attack position, ready to pounce at the slightest movement.

The only movements came from Alexandra and Agnes.

The two possessed women stopped their bloody attacks on each other and walked hand in hand to the edge of the pit. When they reached out, the creature allowed them to touch it. Then it gently brought the green and grey tentacles toward them, slowly wrapping one around each woman.

"We need to hurry," Katrina called to Shirley. She took another swing and sliced through a rope. Shirley followed suit. There were four ropes left, but it didn't matter. They couldn't hold the weight of the enormous bell.

Shirley and Katrina each dove toward the nearest window ledge and held tight despite the slickness of stones from the rainwater.

The remaining ropes snapped like rotted rubber bands. The bell took out the platform they'd been standing on. It plummeted through each successive level.

Down it fell.

THE CREATURE'S MANY EYES SAW IT COMING. IT LET out a shriek as the tentacles around Alexandra and Agnes loosened with a suddenness that made both women lose their balance and totter at the edge of the pit.

Laurence had seen enough death. The women had been wretched these last several days, but he knew it was not of their own volition. They didn't deserve an end like this.

Greater love hath no man than this, that a man lay down his life for his friends. Laurence recited the verse in his mind.

He dove toward them, knocking Alexandra into Agnes and sending both women crashing to the ground slightly away from the edge of the pit. When he came at them, the creature used its tentacles to defend itself, or maybe to defend the women under its control. As it flailed, it smacked against each of the women, sending them rolling farther away from the pit and knocking Laurence into the wet maw below.

Before his head submerged, he managed one glance up toward Kat at the top of the tower, and at the descending bell that would contain the evil.

THE BELL LANDED TRUE. IT CUT SEVERAL outstretched tentacles clean off. Severed, they pulsed and wriggled and then came to a stop, where they dried up and turned to dust in seconds. Agnes and Alexandra came back to themselves on the floor only inches from the rim of the bell. Two nuns remained, though they were bleeding. Their robes were tattered, the whites so bloody that they blended with the black fabrics. Arnie and Rebecca led them to the doorway out of the tower. Herman looked up to see Shirley and Katrina pulling themselves up onto their ledges, where they'd have to hold on carefully until more help arrived.

The evil that had loomed over Raventree Hollow was contained for now, trapped under the bell.

Or so everyone hoped.

Chapter Twenty-Eight

Perhaps the sheriff's office should have been overflowing with residents yelling over each other at Midge Avery and Cal Lincoln behind the administrative desks. The phone should have been ringing off the hook.

Instead, there were only two individuals in the place who weren't employed by the county. One was a strange little man who didn't belong in the town. He was being held in one of the two small cells in the rear annex, which were usually reserved for two town drunks who were pulled in regularly for disturbing the peace in the middle of the night.

In Sheriff Holman's office, though, was a citizen of Raventree Hollow. The sheriff felt like he had to walk on eggshells with this one, since her father was the publisher of the town's sole newspaper. Holman was only a couple of months away from facing reelection—not that there were any competitors for the position, but still. He did not want to jeopardize his good standing with the community, especially not citizens with the power to editorialize the hell out of the events that had occurred in town over the past few days.

"I'm going to ask you again, Ms. Bettencourt, and I want you to really think it through before you answer. What were you and Ms. Givens trying to accomplish by sneaking up to that convent and destroying the bell tower? Did Katrina Givens force you to help her kill Pastor Laurence Wolfram? And how were Ms. Butterfield and Ms. Pennington involved? Your employment with Ms. Butterfield was terminated recently. Were you trying to get revenge on her for firing you?"

Shirley stood up abruptly, knocking her chair over. "I don't know how else I can explain this! That wasn't Agnes and Alexandra up there. Something had—"

"—taken over their minds. Yes. You've said that repeatedly."

"And it's the truth." Shirley hauled the chair back up and plopped down on it with a sigh.

"My deputies and the others sent by the county

have combed through what's left of that bell tower. We didn't see any sign of the monsters you spoke of. The remaining members of the Sisters of Mercy aren't talking—or can't talk, really—and all I'm getting from you and your boyfriend and the McCann kid and Ms. Givens is this monster business. Do you think I can write that down in a report? Do you think your daddy can print that in the newspaper?"

A knock came at the door to Sheriff Holman's office.

"What is it now?" the sheriff shouted.

The door opened slightly, and Cal Lincoln popped his head in.

"I have Bardino here, sir," Cal said.

"Send him in."

Cal pushed the door open the rest of the way and escorted in a small man with a face covered in bruises. He stank, and the stains on his pants indicated that he'd wet himself at some point. Cal handcuffed Danny Bardino's wrists to the arms of the chair next to Shirley before exiting the office.

"Shirley," the sheriff said, "I'd like you to look at this man. Have you seen him before?"

"No, sir, I don't recognize him."

"Mr. Bardino, have you seen this girl before?"

"I haven't," Danny said. He flashed half a pathetic smile at Shirley and then looked away. "I haven't spent time in Raventree Hollow before, as I've told you, Sheriff. This was all just a mistake. A misunderstanding."

"Tell me, then, Bardino, whether this misunderstanding involved monsters controlling your brain. Aliens, perhaps? Leprechauns?"

Bardino chuckled, which turned into a belly laugh. Tears flowed down his face, and he winced at the pain of the salt mixing with the wounds on his cheeks, but he didn't stop laughing until the sheriff asked him to shut up.

"Sorry, sir. No, I haven't seen such creatures. I was just here doing research for my new book." He turned to Shirley. "I'm a writer, you see. I was just trying to understand the mindset of a hit man. Someone offered me money to *off* the coach of your football team. I wasn't gonna do it, honestly!"

"Yes, and even if you'd meant to, you wouldn't have succeeded," Sheriff Holman said with disgust. "Just look at you. You make me sick. Coach Franklin called this morning and said he didn't want to press charges against you. I have too much going on in this town and not enough help, so I will not waste any more time on you, Bardino. I'm going to go make sure the release papers are all ready, and then I want you out of my town forever. If I see you again, you can be sure it won't end as conveniently for you."

With that, the sheriff stood up and grabbed his hat from a rack next to the door.

"So that's it?" Shirley asked. "I can just go?"

"Well, you can stay if you want. I'm heading over to the hospital for the second time today to see if Agnes and Alexandra's painkillers have worn off. Last time, both of them just rambled about not remembering what had happened and not being in control of their own bodies for the last several weeks. By all accounts, they tried to kill each other repeatedly, and yet it seems they're colluding to get out of trouble. I don't get it, but I just want this to be over. I'll give them one chance to change their statements. Otherwise, that's what is going in the official report, and they can live happily ever after together in the psych ward."

Sheriff Holman slammed the door on his way out. Shirley looked again at the man next to her, who flashed her an awkward smile.

"I'm sorry I laughed a minute ago," Danny said. "Sounds like you have quite the imagination. Monsters or whatever."

"I don't care how it sounds," Shirley said. "I know what happened. People died because of it, yet Sheriff Holman has done nothing but mock me."

"Listen, regardless of whether it's true, of course nobody is going to believe it if they didn't see it with their own eyes. It's all about how you frame the story.

People will only believe what they understand. They look for truths in the news that are easy to swallow. If you want to tell a grand story, you've got to go beyond that. Feed it to them through fiction. Write a novel, and they'll expect big, crazy things. Get your story out that way.

"I'll help you out if you're ever interested. I've written a few books myself. Can't say they've made me rich and famous—I mean, just look at me. But at least I can write about all the crazy things I've seen in this world, and nobody thinks of locking me up in the loony bin for it. Just keep a low profile, and this whole thing will blow over for you."

***

SHIRLEY IGNORED THE STARES AND WHISPERS OF everyone she passed on her way down Main Street from the sheriff's office. Her mind was too busy replaying the events of the previous night. It wasn't until someone grabbed her shoulder that she snapped back to reality and took in her surroundings.

"Shirley, thank God you're all right!" It was her father. He'd opened the front door of the *Raventree Herald* office as she passed by in her daze. "Your mother and I tried to get into the sheriff's office to see you earlier this morning, but they wouldn't let anyone in."

He guided Shirley into the building and led her back to his private office. She plopped down on a couch she knew her father slept on almost as often as his bed at home, as he sometimes worked deep into the night getting the next day's edition ready to go to print. It took all of Shirley's strength not to lie back and let her eyes shut.

"Now, Shirl, I'm going to need to hear it all from the beginning. I need to make sure we have the best coverage. You're my number-one source for this story. There are going to be reporters from the big-city papers in town all week, looking for the inside scoop. They're probably waiting on our porch for you to arrive; Sheriff Holman made them leave his office."

Shirley jumped to her feet with energy she didn't realize she still had.

"*The best coverage?*" Shirley said with incredulity. "*Number-one source?* I'm your *daughter*, damn it, and I almost died last night! And all you can think about is your stupid newspaper?"

"Shirl," Hal said, grabbing his daughter's wrist. "If we get this right, I promise I'll bring you on staff like you always wanted. The income this story will bring in will allow us to expand. It's what's best for both of us!"

Shirley shook free of her father's grasp and walked away, slamming his door shut on the way out.

As she walked down the hall toward the front

door, Herman emerged from the tiny darkroom. He blinked rapidly to adjust to the brightness, and a goofy smile came over his face when his vision focused enough to see her.

She threw her arms around him and wept.

Chapter Twenty-Nine
AUTUMN OF 1958

Phillip Winfield had rented out the fairgrounds in the meadow just below his manor. It was the spectacle of a lifetime for the small town of Raventree Hollow. He'd brought in carnival games, musicians who played big band standards, and food catered by all the local restaurants. He'd wanted to hire Alexandra Pennington to take care of the floral arrangements, but she had declined, as her nursery on Main Street was still recovering from the vandalism, so his own gardener Franz had reluctantly taken on the job instead. Phillip had asked the local farmers to bring their finest livestock, and he judged the competitions himself.

The headline event, of course, was the wedding ceremony. The wedding planner—the same gorgeous red-haired woman whose mere presence in the town had sparked an ordeal that could fill a book—ran it with perfection.

There was a moment of silence to kick off the ceremony so all could mourn the man Phillip Winfield had wanted to officiate the wedding. Pastor Laurence Wolfram's replacement asked everyone to bow their heads as he prayed for those affected by the loss of the town's spiritual leader. Shirley turned to her left and took Katrina's hands, while Herman stretched his left arm around both of them and leaned in for the prayer.

During the reception meal, Rebecca and Phillip walked around to greet all the townspeople at their tables.

"Mr. Winfield," said Ronnie Marie, "this is the most beautiful gesture you could have given us after everything that happened in our town. Why did you go to all the trouble?"

"Well," Phillip said, meeting his new bride's eyes and then glancing toward Shirley, Katrina, and Herman, "I've been reminded that there is so much good in Raventree Hollow. I've always heard the stories about my parents and grandparents and great-grandparents being a big part of this town, and of this town being a big part of their lives. I'm a bit shy, and I know I seem like a recluse, but I wanted you all to know how special you've been to my family."

The older women ate up every word uttered by

the handsome groom. They relished his attention, each one grabbing his sleeve, telling him some morsel of information they thought he'd find interesting, and they didn't want to let him go. Rebecca used the opportunity to walk over to the next table, where she embraced Shirley and Katrina.

"They all seem to love him," Rebecca said, smiling over to her new husband. "This whole town adores him."

"You don't know the half of it," Shirley said, surprising herself. She took a quick gulp of champagne, which gave her an extra boost of courage. "I may have had a minor obsession myself, and the photographs on my wall to prove it." She turned to Herman and leaned into him. "But I was a little girl then. My heart belongs somewhere else now."

Rebecca took one of Katrina's hands. "You are all welcome up at the manor anytime you want. We should make a regular time to meet up. The wine selection in Phillip's cellar is unbelievable! We can play some croquet, gossip, tease Phillip, whatever you want."

"That's very kind of you, Rebecca," Katrina said. "I wish I could take you up on it, but I'm putting my home and shop up for sale this week."

"You're leaving Raventree Hollow?"

"I've been here my entire life, and I never fit in with anyone except Laurence. Maybe he was the reason I stayed, hoping we'd find our happily ever after, but of course that didn't happen. There's a much bigger world out there, and I'm finally ready to explore it."

"We should do the same!"

Shirley turned toward Herman, who stared back at her with a look of certainty. "What?" she asked.

"Shirl, you have big dreams with the talent to match. You're a wonderful photographer and writer. You told me you want to tell the story of what happened, but not in the way your father wanted, for his own benefit. You deserve better."

Shirley leaned in and kissed him passionately. When she pulled away, she caught sight of Phillip Winfield. At her age, Shirley's dreams and desires were still constantly changing, but she knew that her earlier obsession had been nothing more than a girlish fantasy. She had grown beyond it.

"You're right, Herman. This place is too small for me—for us. We can make it without my father. Without Raventree Hollow.

"Together."

ALEXANDRA PENNINGTON HAD RECEIVED AN INVITATION, just like the rest of the townspeople. She had pinned it to the corkboard in the kitchen alongside the past-due utility bills, the expired coupons she'd clipped from the Sunday paper, and the grade school photographs she'd received of her cousin Dottie's smug-faced little brats. It was a place where items hung, forgotten, until they yellowed and decayed, or until she ran out of room and needed to tear something off and throw it into the fireplace so she could stab a hole through the next item with a rusting pin.

She had told Kenneth that perhaps she would dig one of her nice dresses out of the back of her closet and do her best to squeeze into it; it had been years since she'd been to a wedding. Women her age were far past their prime, she thought, and it wasn't as if any of her old girlfriends had walked down the aisle in the last decade. And the men her age, with their tobacco-stained teeth and beer-bloated paunches, were no temptation for the gals who had remained single due to choice or circumstance. They weren't at all like her Kenneth.

Alexandra had caught the look of dismay on Kenneth's face when she had finally made up her mind not to go. He'd wanted to use the event as their big coming out as a couple. Kenneth had become good friends with Phillip Winfield over the past few months, sharing the racquetball court at the country club with the wealthy young man on a regular basis. He wasn't going to miss out on the wedding festivities. Alexandra had reminded Kenneth of her recent ordeal and the still-healing bruises that had puffed her face up to what felt like double its normal size. He'd understood, and they'd continued to have their night meetings in secret.

With the rest of the town at the fairgrounds for the reception, Main Street was unusually silent. Alexandra pulled her coat off the rack in her foyer, slipped it on, reached for the doorknob, and hesitated. She'd taken to leaving the house only when the sun went down so she didn't have to see the wreckage of her garden in broad daylight. Kenneth had tried to coax her out, to get her to breathe fresh air and get on with her life, but she hated to consider what the passersby would think of her if she were to toil in her yard in front of them. Today, though, there were no pedestrians making their way up the sidewalk. There were no excuses.

She turned the handle. The door creaked open. Sunlight washed over her.

And the smell.

True, it wasn't the hodgepodge of scents from her garden, her life's work, that had once greeted her in the mornings like a carefully curated potpourri, but there was life in it. There was a budding beauty to it. The essence of a future.

She walked down the porch steps and took in the sights. The flowers weren't blooming yet, not ready for picking. It would be weeks still before she could open her stall with a limited stock, but what she saw filled her with hope. She trotted carefully across the paving stones to the corner where her lilacs had once bloomed. She didn't miss pruning them, but the splash of color they'd added to the garden was still vivid in her mind. She stood over the plot where the shoots of the bush were just starting to poke back through the earth, and she found herself in a daze.

A rustling behind her snapped her out of her frozen state. Without the rosebushes or any of the vines growing up the trellises, she could see clearly across her entire front garden. There was nobody there, and nowhere to hide if there was. But then something caught her eye near the front gate, in the shadow cast by the shuttered booth. She cut through the beds of soil, careful to avoid any rehabilitated plants popping through, and then she saw it.

There, in the one place shielded from the glow of the sun, was the tentacle.

Alexandra sucked in her breath and held it, unable to let it back out. The thing was green, but not the color of any of her plants. It was a sickly reptilian green. She was sure that, had the sun been in a different position in the sky, she'd see the tentacle's tacky sliminess. There was no wind, but the freakish thing swayed. Stretched. Reached for *her*.

"A nice day for gardening."

Alexandra yelped in shock. She turned around and faced Arnie McCann. He looked back at her. It was a knowing look. The boy had seen her at her worst, when she had not been in control of her body or her mind. When she'd looked death in the face and even contributed to deaths herself—the nuns, Pastor Laurence. The boy had been there. He'd helped stop it all.

"Good afternoon, Mr. McCann," Alexandra said after catching her breath. She reached for her face, wanting to cover her bruises, but the boy had already seen everything. She walked out of the shadow of the booth and leaned against her picket fence across from Arnie. "Not off to the wedding with the rest of the Hollow, then?"

"Not my scene," he said. He pushed up his glasses before they escaped his nose. "Going to open up the library in case anyone comes through. Glad to see your garden is starting to bloom again. Take care!"

He was off just as quickly as he'd arrived. Alexandra watched him make his way up Main Street, not because she was interested in his route but to avoid the thing that was waiting for her behind the booth. She took a deep breath, let it out, and turned to face her fear.

An aloe plant sat there, its roots in the soil just where they'd always been planted. No slime. No tentacle moving of its own volition. Just a plant. She looked around at the others popping out of the soil in the autumn sunlight.

There was life budding in Alexandra Pennington's nursery, and it was nothing to be feared.

———

PHILLIP WINFIELD'S HILLTOP ESTATE LOOMED OVER the east side of town. Beyond it was a plot of land normally reserved for the town's annual fair, but it was currently being used as a wedding venue, and what a celebration it looked to be. Agnes Butterfield could see it from her window on the third floor of the Hellman Home for Rehabilitation. As far as she knew, nobody who had ever escaped the asylum had attempted to blend in with the carnies at the fair, nor had they ever climbed the hill to hide amongst the lush gardens of Winfield Manor. It was east they'd headed, down to the train station and away from Raventree Hollow. There, they could sneak into a boxcar and travel halfway across the country before they came out of the spell of whatever medications they'd been administered at Hellman Home.

Agnes had a secret, though. The medications did nothing to her. While her peers sat on their chairs in the common room, strung out and drooling over their unused checkers boards, Agnes only pretended to be like them. She had become quite good at pretending over the last few months, after all—pretending she was in control of her mind, pretending she was in control of her body. She couldn't tell her doctors she was still sharing those vessels with another being. She couldn't confide in any of the lunatics she was locked away with, either. And so Agnes sat in silence, occasionally babbling to reassure the attendants that she was in the same sorry state as her peers.

A phone rang at the desk across the room. Nurse Petra had been assigned to watch the free play session that afternoon, though there wasn't much to watch. The staff always made sure to drug the patients nearly unconscious after lunch so nobody could function, except on days when visitors were expected. Nobody visited Agnes, unless one counted Ronnie Marie. On those days, Agnes *wished* the drugs worked on her so she could drown out the endless babbling of the pathetic woman. Ronnie Marie wasn't visiting that day, however. She was off at the big wedding with everyone else in town.

Some commotion was happening downstairs in the cafeteria, and Nurse Petra was called away to assist the orderlies. Agnes took one quick look around the room, smiled at the collective daze, and locked the door. Without surveillance, she rolled her chair over to the windows that looked to the west to give hope to the inhabitants of Hellman Home that they could one day rejoin society in Raventree Hollow. She looked beyond the prisonlike gates of the facility and across the fields to the large white tents under which the peons of the town were rubbing shoulders with whatever fancy friends Phillip and Rebecca Winfield had invited to their celebration.

She was too far away to make out anyone in particular, but Agnes was certain that wench Shirley Bettencourt was down there, raising a glass of champagne with the witch Katrina Givens. Ronnie Marie was probably biting into her cake alongside Alexandra Pennington. Maybe the surviving nuns had even descended from the ruins of their perch to join the shindig. They were all down there celebrating their pathetic little lives, their newfound peace, their wonderful future together.

Agnes clenched the muscles in her throat. She sucked up phlegm from deep within, brought it up to the back of her tongue, and spat. The thick, greyish-yellow mucus slid slowly down the windowpane, obscuring her view of the wedding reception. She watched as it slithered like a snake.

Like a tentacle.

Like what she knew was growing inside of her.

Agnes Butterfield relocated so she could once again see through a clear windowpane. A giggle escaped her lips as she remembered her fears months ago that the whole town would laugh at her when she'd taken a drunken tumble down the stairs and ended up in Doctor Chou's office.

The giggle turned into a full-on roar of laughter as she looked out at the people of Raventree Hollow and their pathetic little celebration. Behind her, the other patients of Hellman Home joined in. When the orderlies returned, it took another handful of pills to calm everyone. Everyone, that is, but Agnes Butterfield, who cackled all the way back to her padded cell.

An orderly secured one bolt on the heavy door, then a second. It made them all feel safe and secure. Agnes knew, however, that she could break right through the door when the voice inside her head told her it was time.

And so she laughed some more.

Epilogue
AUTUMN OF 1959

Rebecca Winfield's friends weren't willing to make the trip to the small town as often as she had hoped, and the only people in town whom she'd gotten to know had packed up and left months ago.

Her first wedding anniversary with Phillip was coming up, and they'd be traveling to Paris for a week of shopping and spas and fine dining, followed by a cruise down the Riviera. But in the meantime, she'd grown quite lonely at the manor. She'd taken to visiting the wine cellar often. Phillip was too busy running the family business to notice, but she'd grown quite addicted to the feel of the glass at her lips.

The cook, Pierre, had cleaned up after lunch and was taking a well-deserved break in his quarters. He'd surely taken notice of Rebecca's taste for the sweet red, but he never seemed to judge her when she walked past him in the kitchen to reach the cellar stairs.

She descended those steps now in the dim light of a single bulb overhead. At the bottom, she pushed open the door and breathed in the familiar earthy scent of the place. No matter how hot and humid it got in the late summer months above Raventree Hollow, the cellar was always blissfully cool. She flipped the switch, sending an entire row of lightbulbs to life over the long corridor of shelves.

Rebecca didn't know the difference between the years written on the labels or the wineries they came from. She cared much more about the buzz the contents gave her. She ran her fingers along the shelves, not looking for anything in particular, humming an old folk song as she went.

A rumbling sensation stopped her in her tracks.

The bottles clinked in their racks. The lights overhead flickered, then returned to their stable brilliance. Rebecca's song froze in her throat. She listened, bracing herself for another quake. It didn't come.

She picked up the nearest bottle without looking and turned back toward the stairs. When she'd taken three steps, a louder *slam* rang through the cellar. She dropped the bottle, and the glass shattered at her feet. Red wine soaked through her slippers.

Rebecca turned away from the stairs and the mess of glass and fermented grape juice on the floor. She didn't want to go farther down the corridor, but her feet carried her there anyway. With each step, she felt the squelch of the liquid that had soaked through her socks. Little prickles of glass dug into her toes. Blood mixed with the red liquid. Yet she continued her journey.

At the end of the corridor of wine racks, she made a right turn. It was much darker here—the lights weren't as close together. Many bulbs had already met their demise, and those that remained were dim or flickering. This section of the basement was less organized. All around her, chests of old family clothing were strewn about. Moth-eaten fancy furniture, once as costly as automobiles, sat partially covered by mold-stained sheets. Trails of rat droppings lined the baseboards.

Another loud crash. It came from somewhere farther ahead. Rebecca turned another corner and found a staircase descending into yet another subterraneous chamber. She took each stone step carefully, ignoring the pain in her feet; it seemed to reach impossibly far down.

At the bottom, she found herself in what felt like a cave. The next crash echoed loudly from just ahead of her. A single bulb over the stairs provided just a sliver of light.

There in the center of the floor was a large wooden platform. Even in the dimness, she could make out a series of symbols carved into it: a leaf, an eye, a serpent, a sun, a flame, a crescent moon, and a goat's head. The wood was slightly cracked. Bubbles of putrid, dark liquid emerged from the spaces between the boards.

Rebecca turned back toward the stairs. Phillip Winfield stood there, the light at his back, casting a veil of shadows over his face.

"I really wish you hadn't come down here," he said.

Behind Rebecca, a pair of tentacles burst through the wood and flailed toward her.

Winfield Manor sat on the eastern hill, a counterpart to the hill on which the Convent of the Sisters of Mercy had been built for a family lost to time and tragedy. Both structures towered over the small town of Raventree Hollow like watchful sentinels. Or, perhaps, like two predators ready to pounce on their prey.

Down in Raventree Hollow, nobody could hear Rebecca Winfield scream.

For more stories set in Raventree Hollow, check out the series page on Amazon. Signed paperbacks are available directly on my website shop. For exclusive content, news, and discounts, please visit ryanhoytauthor.com and sign up for the newsletter. Be sure to read the rest of the stories that take place in Raventree Hollow, including *Senior Class* and *Butterscotch*.

Also by Ryan Hoyt

HORROR AND DARK FICTION

Senior Class: A Raventree Hollow Story

Pearl and Rosemary are the last of their kind. At 90 years old, death calls for them. Who will be the left standing? A short story chapbook set in the town of Raventree Hollow, this can be read as a standalone tale or enjoyed along with *Raventree Hollow*.

Butterscotch: A Raventree Hollow Story

A family moves into an old home to find the previous owner has left behind a hutch with a candy dish. Aggressive neighbors, a trio of cats, and a hidden purple bag lead the family to seek out answers. "Butterscotch" is a short story chapbook set in the town of Raventree Hollow.

Ditch of the Damned

While traveling with her family across the American frontier, Eudora is pulled off the wagon trail by a sensation deep within her bones. She ignores a warning sign and proceeds toward a hole in the earth in the middle of the wilderness. "Ditch of the Damned" is a short story set in 1847, the latest of the A Machete & Quill Horror line.

Freddy Goodman (Ain't No Good Man)

His coming-of-age story was *so* twenty years ago. So why do the words of that old witch still haunt him? A short story of contemporary fiction with elements of magical realism.

EPIC FANTASY

The Forest of Despair

A heroine's first adventure. A kingdom's last hope. The new female-led epic fantasy series The Aepistelle Chronicles begins here.

The Isle of Abandonment

She once saved a kingdom with her friends. Now she must do it alone. Gemma Calvertson's story continues months after the events of *The Forest of Despair* as she and her friends face their biggest challenges yet.

The Realm Beyond

To help her friends and bring truth to the people of Aepistelle, she must join the ranks of the enemy King Davin and his Royal Mystic Committee. Gemma Calvertson's story ends here.

The Witch of Ferathan

An alluring stranger. A trail of destruction. Will Ferathan survive her charm? *The Witch of Ferathan*, an Aepistelle Chronicles novella, is set seventy-five years before the events of *The Forest of Despair* and can be read as a standalone story.

Acknowledgments

Thank you for reading *Raventree Hollow*. While my first two books were fantasy, I had to deviate to tell this story. As a reader, I regularly hop between genres, whether it is horror, fantasy, or spy thriller, so there was no way I was going to stick with just one genre as a writer. While I plan to continue my fantasy series after this book, I have more horror tales in the works, and I hope you'll stick with me for those.

This story was inspired by my favorite story-tellers: Shirley Jackson and Stephen King. My original concept was Jackson's *The Possibility of Evil* combined with the large town-wide casts of King's *Needful Things* and *Salem's Lot*. I veered from that as I got deeper into the story, but those authors' works are deeply embedded into my heart and mind, so you will still find plenty of influence throughout.

As always, I'm grateful for my wife and kids and the space they sometimes allow me to have so that I can work on my writing projects in little bits at a time. It may have taken two years to get this book from concept to the final printed page, but I did it!

Thanks also to my beta readers, including Muriel Tronc (author of *Call Me, Gwapo* and *Five More Pixs*) and Ky Venn (author of *Justice in Magic*) for providing me with feedback to shape the final telling of this story. Alison Cherry did her magic once again with a copyedit to make this story the best version of itself, and Matt Seff Barnes really brought it all together nicely with the cover.

Please leave a review if you enjoyed the book, and tell your friends and librarians about it. Don't forget to sign up for my newsletter to get free content, exclusive announcements, and more. Thank you.

Ryan Hoyt

P.S. If you want to buy my books in any digital or physical format, please consider buying directly from my website, ryanhoytauthor.com/shop. Thanks!